"You're playing with fire...."

Curiously enough, Mel didn't ask herself if she wanted Pete.

She just exulted in the power of him wanting her.

She had a red-blooded man in a tuxedo who was very happy to be with her right now. And they had a beach all to themselves.... Except it wasn' so private, what with the hundred-odd window looking down at them from the hotel.

Mel brushed those concerns aside for the moment—she'd just have to get him to his hote room. For now, she had her hand on the prize. She squeezed him gently through his pants and Pete groaned.

"Mel," he said hoarsely, "you really shouldn't be doing that."

Mel used her other hand to ease down his zipper. "Show me what you've got."

Pete made a strangled sound in the back of his throat. "Melinda, you're killing me!"

She smiled. "I know. But you'll die happy."

Dear Reader,

I'm sure you've heard the saying, You can't please all of the people all of the time. And most of us, at some point, have felt that we can't please anyone, at any time.

I was in a hotel registration line, witnessing a clerk gracefully accept abuse from a woman who clearly thought she was the disrespected empress of her own universe, when I got the idea for Pete Dale's character. What would it be like to have a job that involved trying to keep people happy all day long?

Pete, the hero of *Bringing Home a Bachelor,* works at a luxury hotel with very picky customers. His job is to bring in more business, and therefore more money. But trying to please his customers, his boss, his good friend the groom, the woman he loves *and* her dragon of a mother—all at the same time—is a recipe for disaster!

Poor, professionally polite Pete has to take a stand, and it's not one he's comfortable with: No More Mr. Nice Guy…at least when it comes to the people who are making his girlfriend Melinda's life impossible.

I hope you'll enjoy reading *Bringing Home a Bachelor* as much as I enjoyed writing it, as well as the two previous books in the All the Groom's Men series— *Borrowing a Bachelor* and *Blame it on the Bachelor.*

All the best,

Karen Kendall

Karen Kendall

BRINGING HOME A BACHELOR

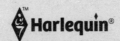

TORONTO NEW YORK LONDON
AMSTERDAM PARIS SYDNEY HAMBURG
STOCKHOLM ATHENS TOKYO MILAN MADRID
PRAGUE WARSAW BUDAPEST AUCKLAND

ISBN-13: 978-0-373-79690-8

BRINGING HOME A BACHELOR

ABOUT THE AUTHOR

Karen Kendall is an author of more than twenty novels and novellas for several publishers. She is a recipient of awards such as the Maggie, the Book Buyer's Best, the Write Touch and *RT Book Reviews* Top Pick, among others. She grew up in Austin, Texas, and has lived in Georgia, New York and Connecticut. She now resides in south Florida with her husband, two greyhounds, a cat...and lots of fictional friends! She claims to have real ones, too. She loves hearing from readers! Please visit her website at www.KarenKendall.com.

Books by Karen Kendall

To get the inside scoop on Harlequin Blaze and its talented writers, be sure to check out blazeauthors.com.

All backlist available in ebook. Don't miss any of our special offers. Write to us at the following address for information on our newest releases.

Harlequin Reader Service
U.S.: 3010 Walden Ave., P.O. Box 1325, Buffalo, NY 14269
Canadian: P.O. Box 609, Fort Erie, Ont. L2A 5X3

1

WHAT A MONDAY. The clock said it was only 9:45 a.m., and Pete Dale, senior account manager for Miami's Playa Bella Hotel, had already put out three customer-relations fires by the time his office phone rang ominously for the fourth time.

He squinted at the phone suspiciously, rubbed his temples and sighed. Who was calling now? The cantankerous, octogenarian charity-ball chairwoman? The pain-in-the-butt, preppy pro-golfer's rep? Or the charming, chin-wagging Chilean who loved to chat for hours about every detail of his upcoming fiftieth anniversary dinner for two hundred?

Pete had jumped at the job with Playa Bella two years ago because it enabled him to return to the sun, sand and sea of Miami. But paradise had its price.

He picked up the receiver and held it to his still-burning ear—Playa Bella's spa had managed to offend a Latin American dictator's wife, and her secretary had just given him what-for. "Pete Dale. May I help you?"

"Pete!" A voice boomed like a cannon into his brain. But he didn't mind, because it was the voice of a friend. His oldest friend, to be exact. He'd known Mark since junior high.

"Mark, my man," Pete said with relief. "How are you?" He

grinned and leaned back in his leather chair, letting his head loll to the side. "You ready for this weekend?"

Mark was getting married in five days, and Pete and the rest of the groomsmen had wild plans for him first. There was no bachelor party like a Miami-based bachelor party— they planned to put *The Hangover* to shame, though without actually losing their groom in the process.

"I'm ready—the question is, is Kendra?" Mark laughed.

"Nobody could be prepared to take you on for life," Pete ribbed him.

"True. Very true. Listen, I called for a couple of reasons. One, to say hi. Two, er…you remember my sister Melinda, right?"

"Of course I remember Melinda." Pete shifted in his chair.

He'd gotten a real shock when he'd run into her at a Dolphins game a couple of years back. Hadn't recognized her. Though she'd looked familiar, he couldn't place her. A tumble of dark hair, a sunburned nose, big blue eyes, and a curvaceous body made for a man's pleasure.

She'd glanced at him, then turned to walk away with her friends. He'd been openly admiring her rounded ass and wondering what it would feel like in his hands, when she'd turned back toward him and stared, hard.

Busted, Pete pretended that he'd been searching for something.

Then she'd put a hand on his arm and said, in tones of disbelief, "Pete? Pete Dale, is that really you?"

He'd raised his ogling eyes and looked at her face again, puzzled. Where had he seen her before?

"Pete, I'm Melinda. Melinda Edgeworth. Mark's sister."

Shame flared in his gut as heat climbed his neck. "Mel? No way…oh, my God, it is you."

He registered with surprise that she was blushing, too. Of course she was! He'd been fixated on her ass, pervert that he was, and she knew it. Oh, hell. "You're all grown up," he added, instantly wishing that he could take back the lame words.

She shrugged. "How are you?"

"Uh, great. You?"

And then her friends had hustled her away, before he could think to get her number. Not that he should have. Mel was Mark's little sister, which put her strictly off-limits.

Mark's next words brought Pete back to the present with a jolt.

"Melinda doesn't have a date for the wedding, and I wanted to ask you if you'd, well, make sure she has a good time."

"Sure, no problem," Pete said easily.

"You're the only nice guy of my acquaintance, and you know how it is with Mel," Mark said.

No, How was it?

"If she'd just lose that baby fat of hers, her life would be different."

Baby fat? Pete frowned, sat up straight in his chair and settled his elbows on his desk. "Oh, come on. Mel's a very pretty girl."

"Uh, huh," Mark said, in dismissive tones. "You know, Kendra tried to give her some advice on how to eat, but it didn't go over too well."

Pete felt a quick wave of sympathy for Mel. Kendra was so thin that he wasn't sure she even qualified for a size at all. He was pretty sure he'd heard of women who were actually size zero. Kendra's legs looked like chopsticks, if you asked him, and her arms were toothpicks. She looked downright brittle; as if she'd break in half if she so much as stubbed a toe. Mark was lucky that she hadn't punctured his kidneys in the night, with one of her elbows.

Put them side by side, Kendra and Melinda, and Pete'd take Mel any day of the week. She had beautiful skin, bright eyes, shiny dark hair that was always escaping the clip she wore to hold it back. And oh yeah, there were those abundant curves of hers.

Pete personally had never been a fan of the South Beach Swizzle Sticks that Mark had collected in college. And they tended to be low-energy and moody, since they were malnourished.

"Well, anyway. The family's been a little worried about Mel lately. Something happened with a big account at the bakery last week—she won't talk about it—and she's been holed up in her shell, doing nothing but work. So if you'd just—I don't know—get her out on the dance floor for a few numbers…well, I'd really appreciate it."

"No problem," Pete said again. "Mel is a very cool girl and I'd be delighted."

"You don't have a date to the wedding either, right, bud?"

Pete gritted his teeth. "No, Mark, I don't."

"That's what Mom and Kendra said—that you were coming stag."

Thanks, Mom and Kendra. Appreciate it. No need to rehash why he was coming alone—that he'd been unceremoniously dumped by his wine-distributor girlfriend a month before. For the hotel manager of an entire cruise line.

Yes, Maribel mixed business and pleasure very well indeed, and he'd just been too stupid to realize that she'd move on when she found a guy a few pay grades and career notches above him.

"So that's perfect, then," continued Mark.

"Yep. Perfect." Pete was nothing if not agreeable. It was part of his job, part of his personality. It sucked sometimes, being a Certified People Pleaser, but placating various warring family members had set him on that course long ago.

So when Pete felt like telling people to take a flying leap, he generally stuffed his emotions and smiled instead. He offered to give them a courtesy discount, no matter how discourteous they'd been to him. He jollied them into a better mood. He sent them complimentary champagne and fruit baskets.

Pete hotly denied, though, that he was a member of the subspecies Doormaticus. Nor was he a butt-kisser or a toady. He was simply a customer-relations expert. He kept the peace, and there was nothing wrong with that, was there?

Pete handled situations with his trademark easy smile, a professional grade eye-twinkle and a voice carefully modulated to Soothe/Empathize on his Internal Customer Service Dial.

Everybody loved Pete…with the evident exception of his ex, Maribel.

Mark had called her a witch. Their fraternity brother Adam, a medical student, had said Pete was well-rid of her. And Dev, another fraternity brother, had offered to love-her-and-leave-her in a one-night-stand of revenge on his friend's behalf.

Pete had politely declined this generous offer of male solidarity and explained to Dev that even he, as a former rock 'n' roll stud who still owned leather pants, couldn't compete with the hotel manager of a cruise line—at least not in terms of business opportunities for Maribel.

"I don't hold anything against her," Pete told him. "It's just her nature."

Dev had coughed. "I don't hold anything against scorpions, either, dude—but I still step on 'em."

Pete couldn't help a snort of amusement at that, but he quickly banished it in favor of feeling magnanimous towards Maribel, and therefore superior. That really helped with the whole lovelorn depression thing.

"So," Mark boomed, "I'll see you guys Thursday night, then!"

"Yes, you will…though you probably won't see us in focus for very long, my man. After a few shots, you'll be seeing two of everyone."

"I'm not sure I can handle seeing two of Dev," Mark said, sounding a little alarmed.

Pete laughed.

"And don't hurt me too bad, or Kendra will be pissed."

"Why don't we manage that possibility from the get-go," Pete suggested. "Do not make any lunch plans with your bride for the next day."

THE MORNING WAS NOT receding, no matter how much Melinda Edgeworth wished it to. In fact, the Miami sun was rising into the sky as cheerfully as it always did; defying her and shining down upon her lazy, moping self.

She wanted it to immolate her like a vampire so that she wouldn't have to face her bakery and work. Tomorrow she had to deliver three hundred fresh chocolate croissants and three hundred vanilla raspberry scones to a medical convention, which meant that she and Scottie, her assistant, had to make them today.

That, in addition to a groom's cake, an elaborate baby-shower cake, and a large order of petits fours for high tea at a ladies' club.

Noooooo! Melinda closed her eyes again and groaned. She felt the small, warm body against hers stir. Mami, her little Schipperke mix, got to her tiny, fuzzy feet and yawned, sending a wave of hot dog-breath up Mel's protesting nostrils.

Melinda opened one eye. "You have the breath of a camel, sweetheart."

Mami yipped, climbed onto Mel's chest and licked her face with gusto.

"That wasn't an invitation to make me smell like a camel,

too." But Mami was irresistible, and knew it. Mel scooped her up, kissed her head, and tucked her under her chin.

Mami tolerated this treatment for a couple of minutes, but then wriggled free, yipping for her breakfast.

"Not open for business yet," Mel grumbled. She rolled onto her stomach and stuffed her head under her pillow. At least she had her brother's four-tiered wedding cake done. But there was so much else to tackle.

Get out of bed this instant and don't be a whiner, said her Inner Drill Sergeant. *You're lucky you get to play with ganache and fondant and don't have to work in a coal mine.*

God, she hated her Inner Drill Sergeant. Why couldn't he strangle to death in a loop of her small intestine? Or fall into a pit of digestive acid?

Twenty minutes later, Mami had her heart's desire out of a can, while Melinda sat at her breakfast table, deeply committed to smothering her Inner Drill Sergeant in pancakes, butter, syrup and bacon. Lots of bacon, crispy, the way she liked it.

She pictured the Sergeant being pelted by the mouthfuls of food as she swallowed them. "That'll teach you to nag me about work ethic and calories and exercise," she muttered.

But it didn't shut him up, of course.

No, he just asked her nastily whether she was finished yet, or whether she wanted to add another thousand calories to her breakfast—a third of a pound. He told her she was a disgrace. He told her that she was fat…

Just like Franco Gutierrez had, last week, when she'd smacked him for snaking a hand down her pants and fondling her bare butt. She'd chased him out of her shop with a rolling pin, instead of compromising her ethics in order to keep his very large Java Joe's account.

Gorda! He'd spat at her. *Cow!* This was followed by something filthy in Spanish. The implication was that she'd be lucky if he deigned to 'do' her. Who was she to turn him down?

But she had, and it was going to seriously hurt her in financial terms. Java Joe's, a big café chain, supplied almost twenty-five percent of her income. How was she going to replace it? She couldn't go to her aunt Kylie at Sol Trust again. Kylie had made her the initial bank loan for the start-up after Mel had graduated from culinary school and hung out her shingle as a pastry chef, but her condo was at stake as collateral. And she had to generate enough income to pay all expenses, plus her mortgage, her bills and installments on the debt.

Mel stopped eating and dropped her fork. Then she pushed her plate away, leaned her head on her arms and wondered miserably why she could run a busy high-end bakery, but lacked the competence to run her own body in the way she knew she should.

She picked up Mark and Kendra's engagement photo and found her eyes watering at Mark's expression of pure love for his bride.

Amazing. He hadn't looked like that when he'd painted Mel's Barbie with Barbiecue sauce—ha, ha—and broiled her in Mom's oven in her pageant gown and tiny rubber shoes; or when he and Pete Dale had buried Mel up to her neck in sand and kept her there on the beach for hours, only letting her drink from a plastic water-gun aimed at her mouth.

She shook her head as she thought about the teenaged Pete, about the huge crush she'd had on him back then. She'd turned bright red every time he came near her, and either stuttered or—on one horrifying occasion—burped convulsively when she tried to speak to him.

She hadn't seen Pete in years, except for the brief sighting at that Dolphins' game, but he'd be at the wedding, of course.

She ignored the brief flutter of her pulse and stared at Mark's engagement photo again.

Her brother certainly hadn't worn that expression of tenderness when he and Pete had removed the ladder from the edge of the tree house, leaving her stranded long past dinnertime.

And what Kendra saw in him, she wasn't entirely sure. But then again, Mel was his sister, and had grown up with him. She'd seen the crusty dishes, dirty clothes and hidden, gross girlie magazines in his boyhood room.

Melinda liked Kendra. She did. Kendra had a good heart, even though Mel didn't know how there was room for it in that tiny chest cavity of hers.

She was happy for Mark.

So why did she feel like moping in a corner? She pondered that question, which she couldn't seem to answer.

You're afraid nobody will ever look at you the way Mark is looking at Kendra, supplied her Inner Drill Sergeant. *And you know why you're afraid of that? Because you're fat!*

Melinda reached for the plate of pancakes again.

My self-esteem is not dependent on my weight, Sarge. So what if I'm not a human twig? And besides, I don't care what you say. You're only a figment of my imagination.

But in spite of her tough retort, he'd gotten to her, as the voice behind years of subconscious programming by fashion magazines, television and movies. And his message was: you're not desirable unless you're thin.

Mel added more syrup to her plate and finished every bite of the pancakes. She only hoped she would fit into her bridesmaid's dress on Saturday.

2

MELINDA EDGEWORTH HAD vanished—bridesmaid dress, pearls, up-do and all—and she hadn't even had the courtesy to leave a glass slipper lying around as a clue to her whereabouts.

Pete hunted for Mel in the posh wedding crowd at Playa Bella, with no success. She'd disappeared faster than a Swedish meatball down the gullet of a guest.

He accounted for the other four bridesmaids, who were easy to spot in their matching turquoise gowns, but Melinda wasn't among them.

Not a good sign. Pete frowned, recalling even through the fog of his continuing hangover what he'd promised Mark: to make sure his little sister had a good time at the wedding.

Mark and Kendra had tied the knot in a beautiful ceremony less than an hour ago. The photographer had rounded up all the groomsmen, including Pete, and taken a goofy shot of them admiring Kendra's ring. Then he'd rounded up all the bridesmaids, including Melinda, and taken an equally goofy shot of them in a gaggle around Mark with the blue garter that was now, presumably, back around Kendra's thigh.

After that, Melinda had gone missing.

Pete lurked outside the ladies' room for a couple of minutes, with no luck. Then he tried dialing her room in the hotel, but nobody answered. Finally he dug another couple of ibuprofen out of his pocket, swallowed them dry, and ducked out the back doors.

It was like stepping into a postcard of sunset, sand and ocean waves. The Hotel Playa Bella was located, true to its name, on the beach—on a tiny private key in downtown Miami. That meant the beach, too, was private and open only to guests of Playa Bella. Since Pete worked there in account management, and was specifically in charge of new business development, he'd been able to cut Mark and Kendra quite a deal.

Pete put a hand up to his bleary eyes—God, what had possessed the groomsmen to do all those shots last night?— and looked out towards the water. Sure enough, he spotted a turquoise-draped figure with a brunette updo, walking in the sand with her shoes in her left hand.

"Mel?" Pete called, but he knew it was futile. No way could she hear him over the wind. He looked down at his shiny formal shoes, then back at the sand, and groaned. He sat down on a deck chair and untied his laces, slipped off the shoes and peeled off his socks. He rolled up his pants to his knees and headed after her.

The ocean breeze had picked up, and the force of it plastered his shirt to his chest as he approached her. It also did things to Melinda's dress that he couldn't help appreciating. The flimsy fabric clung to her curves like plastic wrap, and he got a very intimate look at her generously proportioned, sexy derriere.

It was wrong of him to look. Mel was Mark's kid sister, the pudgy little girl that they'd buried to the neck in the sand, petrified with ghost stories and trapped in the old tree house when they'd stolen the ladder…

But look Pete did. And the closer he got, the more he liked what he saw. He hadn't noticed her body at all during the rehearsal dinner—she'd worn something shapeless and forgettable—but the turquoise bridesmaid dress was also fitted at the waist, and more than a little snug in the bust area.

She seemed to sense his gaze on her, because as he approached she turned toward him, and he was faced with a heavenly eyeful of deep, shadowy cleavage. Her breasts strained against the fabric that confined them, and he himself strained mightily not to look at them.

He failed.

Her face became pink as she said, "Hi, Pete. What are you doing out here?"

Heat rose in his own face. "Looking for you."

"Why?" she asked.

He shrugged. "I was going to ask you to dance."

"Me?" Mel swung a champagne bottle out of the folds of her skirt and lifted it towards her lush, pink mouth as Pete raised his eyebrows. She drank, her lips kissing the bottle. He watched the liquid pour into her mouth from inside the dark green glass, the sight erotic as hell. His own mouth went dry.

Little sister. Mark. Again, he had to remind himself.

"What's the matter, Pete?" she asked, throatily. "You've never seen a girl drink from the bottle before?"

"Uh," he said stupidly, around a tongue that felt thick and woolly. "Would you like a glass?"

"No, thanks." She smiled at him. "It would spoil my whole Barefoot Bohemian Bridesmaid thing."

"Oh. I get it," said Pete, who didn't.

Yeah…that was another oddity. Melinda Edgeworth wasn't at all bohemian. Not the sort of girl you'd find wandering a beach barefoot, slugging back booze from a bottle. And yet here she was. Looking like a whole lot of big, blue-eyed trouble, with her updo acting like voodoo on him.

For somehow, over the years, Mel's freckles had faded and

her huge blue eyes—he remembered, with shame, how they'd called her Bug-Eyes—now fit her lovely face.

"Want some?" Mel asked, extending the bottle to him.

Pete took it, touched his lips to where hers had just been, and drank. The wine was cold, dry and effervescent. He felt his hangover stir sleepily and pull the new alcohol over it like a blanket. Yeah, that was it: a little hair of the dog would cure everything…and he'd just drown this sudden, unwelcome and inappropriate lust of his for Melinda.

She walked a couple of paces ahead of him, then bent down to pick up a small sand dollar. The fabric of her dress molded, once again, to that curvy backside of hers, and if she wasn't wearing a thong, then his name was Abraham Lincoln and not Peter S. Dale.

Pete barely restrained a groan.

Mel stood up with her prize and smiled. "It's beautiful, isn't it? So amazing that nature can create something so perfect."

He nodded and held out the champagne bottle, but almost dropped it when Melinda slipped the sand dollar into her cleavage. She took the bottle without noticing that he'd practically started drooling.

"That gives me an idea," she said. "I'm going to make pies that look like sand dollars…and cookies that look like starfish. Maybe cakes shaped like fish, too. It's a perfect theme for Miami."

"How about suns and boats?" Pete suggested.

"Great idea." Mel upended the champagne bottle again, drinking deeply. "I'm going to make it, Pete, no matter what anyone says."

He drew his eyebrows together. "Of course you are. Why would anyone doubt that you're going to be a success?"

Pete noted with alarm that a good three-quarters of the bottle was gone.

"You wouldn't believe," she said, after finally taking a breath, "how many demeaning comments I got while I was enrolled at the Culinary Institute."

"What do you mean?"

"Pastry chef?" Mel mock-scoffed. "Oh-what-cute-cupcakes-you'll-make-for-your-kids-one-day." Up went the bottle again. Glug, glug.

Pete's radar detected deep wounds hidden under Mel's words and consumption of champagne. "Who said that to you?"

The wind had blown a stray lock of hair free and into her face. Mel attempted to blow it back into place, but failed. "My brother Mark, for one. And my dad asked me if I could really support myself by baking cakes and pies."

Pete had been ready with a rejoinder about what a jerk the comment-maker was, but he shut his mouth. "I'm sure they don't mean to be unsupportive."

"Right," she said. Glug.

"So what about your mom?"

"My mom doesn't take it seriously either, but she does order lots of cakes for her friends' birthdays and other occasions."

Melinda was perilously close to finishing off the bottle of champagne. Her speech wasn't slurred, but Pete noted that every time the tide came in, she leaned backward a little. And every time the water rushed away again, she leaned forward, unconsciously echoing its rhythms. Her face had begun to flush, too, because of the alcohol.

Pete deduced that she'd drunk the champagne very quickly, and that more of its effects were going to creep up and clobber her any moment now. Time for a little friendly interference. "Hey, Bug-Eyes," he teased. "Give me some of that."

She narrowed her eyes at him, but handed over the bottle. "I could have lived without being called that ever again, you know."

Pete winked and gave her a friendly shrug. He took two large gulps and k.o.'d the champagne. Then he set the bottle in the sand and manfully restrained a belch.

"Do you know what a complex you and Mark gave me? I went crying to my parents and begged them to take me to the eye doctor so he could fix the problem! I had nightmares about becoming a fly—and no, I never saw the movie because I was afraid to."

Pete struggled mightily to look sympathetic and suitably remorseful, but he burst out laughing instead. "I'm sorry," he gasped.

To his relief, Mel began to laugh, too. "It's not funny," she exclaimed.

"Yes it is," he said, backing away with his palms in the air in case she tried to smack him.

"Well, it wasn't funny at the time!"

He got control over himself and tried to imagine how scary it would be to a six-year-old to wake up in the middle of the night, in the dark, terrified that she'd sprout several hairy insect legs and a pair of wings to go with her existing "bug eyes."

Regret washed over him. "Mel, I'm truly sorry if we said anything to traumatize you back then. We were just a couple of dumb kids."

"It was years ago," she said dismissively. "Forget it."

"Okay."

She picked up the empty bottle and peered into it. "Hey! You drank all the champagne."

Pete decided not to correct her, though he'd had approximately one-eighth of the bottle and she'd had the rest.

"That's not very nice."

"What can I say? I'm not a nice guy." He grinned at her.

She frowned back. "Yes, you are. You weren't always nice as a kid, but now you're so nice that your picture's next to the word in the dictionary."

He found that he was mildly offended. "Not true."

"It is, too. You took off your shoes and came all the way out here to talk to me."

"I came to talk to you because I like you, not because I'm nice."

"You said you wanted to dance with me."

"Yeah…?"

"Well, that proves that you're nice."

"No, it doesn't," Pete said.

"Does too."

"Does not."

This was ridiculous—they were behaving like little kids.

"I wanted to dance with you because you're a beautiful, sexy woman," Pete told her.

Mel snorted and turned away. "Riiiight."

He put a hand on her arm and tugged her back around to face him. "You are. What's with the horse noise?"

Mel's face, already flushed with alcohol, deepened a couple of shades. "Pete, I'm not one of Playa Bella's high-roller clients. You don't have to suck up to me."

Stung, he opened his mouth to make an uncharacteristic retort. Then he saw the shimmer of tears in her eyes and stopped himself.

"I want some more champagne," she said.

"Don't you think you've had enough?"

"Not nearly."

He shrugged. "Okay. I'll get us some more in a minute. What's got you so upset, Mel?"

"Nothing."

"What's Nothing's last name? I'll go beat him up for you," he said teasingly.

"You're going to coldcock my mother?"

Pete winced. "Okay, maybe not. So what did she do, honey?"

Mel expelled a long, quivering breath.

He waited for her to take another and blow that one out, too, staying quiet, not pressuring her to share. Pete knew how to listen. He was a pro. He listened to litanies of complaints from picky customers all day long. He then listened to staff complain about the complaints, as a matter of fact. So whatever Melinda had to say wasn't going to faze him.

"My mother." Mel laughed softly. "My stick-thin mother and her backhanded compliments…"

Uh-oh.

"She told me how lovely the cake looked—the wedding cake I did for Mark and Kendra. And in the same breath she said my life would be so different if I did something outside the 'realm of temptation,' the 'calorie-rich' environment of my bakery."

Pete hissed in a breath. Ouch.

"Yeah, nice, huh?"

"It probably just came out wrong," he said, trying to make her feel better.

She rounded on him. "Oh, so there's a right way to say that?"

"Noooo, maybe not."

"I'm really good at what I do! I'm proud of it!" Two angry tears overflowed Melinda's eyes and rolled down her cheeks.

"Of course you are." Pete wrapped his arms around her and tucked her head under his chin. He rubbed her back and tried very hard not to notice how good her hair smelled— like camellias—or how her breasts mounded solidly against his chest, or how his body reacted to her dangerous curves.

"Then why doesn't my own family take me seriously?" She sniffled against his tuxedo jacket. "My dad still asks me if I need money. My mom treats me like a wayward teenager, and she recently subscribed me to Weight Watcher's online without permission. And Mark only let me do his wedding cake because it was free."

"That cake is stunning," Pete said with honesty, but also because he needed to distract himself. Part of him was hardening, and unfortunately it wasn't his heart.

He prayed that Melinda wouldn't notice. They'd been kids together. She was Mark's baby sister. He couldn't, wouldn't, pop a woody. Not here, not now.

He cleared his throat as she lifted her face from his tuxedo jacket. "Thanks, Pete. You're such a good guy." She hugged him wholeheartedly. "Just for that, you get a free birthday cake."

How about a free birthday suit? Yours?

His body loved that idea.

Oh, hell. Pete closed his eyes.

Houston, we have a problem: the missile has launched.

Melinda stiffened, staring fixedly at the third button on his starched shirt for a beat too long.

She'd noticed. Of course she had.

As if to make sure she'd actually felt his wayward cock pressing into her abdomen, she shifted against him again.

Heat climbed Pete's neck and burst into his cheeks. He took a deep breath. His instinct was to shove her away from him, but it might hurt her already wounded feelings…not to mention that it would leave him exposed, with a telltale tent at his crotch.

So Pete babbled instead. "Absolutely gorgeous, that cake. You made it yourself? How do you get the icing so smooth? How do you make those perfect roses?"

He knew he was asking too many questions, and asking them too fast.

Mel raised her eyes from the oh-so-fascinating button and

met his gaze. Then she moved a hand down his side, trailing it downwards to his upper thigh.

Pete swallowed hard.

No way. Mel had been brought up in a conservative household, and she wouldn't…unfortunately…act on this. It wasn't going to happen, no matter how eager his trouser snake was. She'd had a lot of champagne, true, but—

Nah. Forget it. Not gonna happen.

Then Melinda stepped back two inches and wrapped her fingers around his colossal erection, squeezing it lightly through his trousers.

His mouth fell open.

"Do you really want to hear about how I make roses out of icing, Pete? Or would you like me to help you with this, instead?"

3

SOMETHING DEEP INSIDE Mel exulted, as she stood there on the beach with the wind making a mess of her hair. The tight fit of her satin bridesmaid dress felt sexy now, instead of confining, uncomfortable and embarrassing. She felt…voluptuous.

Pete wanted her. His body had betrayed him. He didn't think of her as a stupid kid anymore, as Bug-Eyes, Mark's little brat of a baby sister. He didn't think of her as fat.

After the week she'd had, after her experience with Franco Gutierrez and a revisit of all her teenage emotional scars, Mel viewed this as a gift.

Curiously enough, she didn't ask herself if she wanted him. She just exulted in the power of him wanting her.

She had a red-blooded man in a tuxedo with a raging erection—and they had a beach all to themselves…except it wasn't so private, what with the hundred-odd windows looking down at them from the vast, modern hotel.

And then there was the question of the two pairs of Spanx she'd donned under the turquoise dress: an instant mood killer.

Mel brushed those concerns aside for the moment—she'd just have to get him to his hotel room. For now, she had her hand on the prize. She squeezed gently and Pete groaned.

"Mel," he said hoarsely, "you really shouldn't be doing that."

She peered up at him from under her lashes. "Why not?"

"Because you're playing with fire, little girl."

An old-fashioned line, but she liked it. Nobody had called her a little girl for a long time. She considered the width of Pete's shoulders and the breadth of his chest. He was only about five-eleven to her five-five, but he was built like the linebacker he'd been in high school. They'd called him Fozzie, since even back then he'd been a big teddy bear of a guy.

Mel used her other hand to ease down his zipper. "Show me what you've got." She pushed aside the fabric of his boxers and cupped him, running her fingers up and down the satiny skin of his cock.

Pete made a strangled sound in the back of his throat. "Melinda, you're killing me!"

She smiled. "I know. But you'll die happy."

He gritted his teeth and looked down at her, shaking his head. "Last chance to run, honey. Last chance to rethink this, before—"

She rubbed the underside of him with her thumb. "Before what?"

"Before you get a whole lot of Pete."

"I think I'd like that."

"Then get your hand out of my pants and take my room key." He dug into his pocket and produced it, sliding it into her palm. "Meet me upstairs. I'm going to use my jacket as a shield, if you know what I mean, and I'll stop to get us another bottle of champagne. Okay?"

She nodded.

He stuffed himself back into his pants and zipped up, carefully.

"If you change your mind, Mel, it's okay."

She stood on tiptoe and kissed him full on the mouth,

drinking in the outdoorsy scent of his aftershave, sliding her hand along the slight bristle of his cheek. "I won't change my mind," she said.

"I sure as hell hope not." Pete eyed her as if she were a cupcake and he a starving diabetic.

She started to turn, but he caught her arm.

"Do me a favor and stand there for a second." He shrugged out of his tuxedo jacket and folded it strategically over his arm. "I don't want to run into any other guests with this battering ram extended out in front of me…"

Melinda laughed at the image. "Does that mean you really want to get inside my castle?"

"Honey, you have no idea," he muttered. "Now go, before I throw you down right here in the sand and have my way with you." Pete winked at her.

Mel picked up the shoes she'd dropped and made a beeline for the hotel, picking her way over the beach barefoot. She was conscious of the fact that Pete was staring after her with lust in his eyes, and a strange, unaccustomed joy bubbled up within her.

Pete thought that she, Melinda, was hot.

Smiling from ear to ear, she put an extra wiggle in her step, just to torture him a little.

She reached the glass French doors of the hotel, pulled one open and ran smack into her mother.

"Melinda! Where have you been?" Jocelyn Edgeworth, elegant and pristine in a powder-blue suit and taupe heels, swept her gaze over Mel, stopping first on her tousled hair, then at the drops of perspiration that dotted her neck and cleavage and finally at her sand-encrusted bare feet. True to form, she flattened her lips and said nothing critical aloud. She let her steel-blue eyes do the talking for her.

Because she didn't voice her opinion, Melinda couldn't possibly make a rude retort. "Walking on the beach," she said.

Jocelyn sighed. "Your brother and Kendra haven't even cut the cake yet!"

"I needed some air. And I've seen the cake. Up close. For hours. I don't need to see it again."

"Wouldn't you like to mingle with the guests? Great-uncle Ernie was just asking about you."

"Great-uncle Ernie is a sweetie, but he's getting senile. I spent half an hour talking with him at the rehearsal dinner last night."

"Well, don't you want some food? There are several low-calorie options…"

"Mom, I'm actually not feeling so well," she lied. "My stomach is upset. I'm going to go up and lie down for a little while."

"I'm sorry to hear that." Jocelyn reached for her hand, but since it was clutching Pete's room key, Melinda tucked it into her skirts and gave her mother a peck on the cheek instead.

"I'll be fine. I'll take a couple of antacid pills and come down to the reception again soon, okay?"

"Well, all right." The steel-blue eyes held motherly concern, but also a bit of irritation. In Jocelyn's book, a little tummy-upset was something to be swallowed and tolerated with a social smile, not indulged or complained about.

If her ancestors hadn't come over on the Mayflower, then they'd arrived shortly afterward, probably swimming in relays behind it. They were all angular, lean, fast-muscle-twitch sorts of people; tennis-players, skiers, marathon runners.

Melinda took after her father's side of the family. "I'll see you in a little while," she said, her brief euphoria and champagne buzz fading fast. She made for the elevator. A glance backward found Jocelyn staring with disapproval at the sand trail made by her bare feet.

As the doors closed and the car carried her upward toward room 817, Melinda no longer felt sexy. She felt like a human sausage squeezed into the two pairs of Spanx. She felt wind-blown and sticky and hopeless. How could a brief encounter with her mother and her prominent, Anglo-Saxon hip bones do this to her?

The elevator reached the eighth floor with a ding and Mel had to decide whether or not to get out. Whether or not to go to Pete's room. Whether or not to wriggle out of the horrible Spanx and expose herself to his gaze.

Just as she hit the button for her own floor, five, the doors opened to reveal a bellhop with a large cart and three other waiting people. Clearly they all wanted to get into the elevator, and equally clearly, if they did there would be no room for her.

"Ma'am?" The bellhop smiled at her and held the door open. Reluctantly, Mel got out, and everyone else got in.

Slowly she made for room 817 and what was probably a huge mistake. Had she really reached out and put her hand on Pete Dale's equipment?

She had.

And squeezed it?

She winced.

And unzipped his pants?

Oh, God. What had she been thinking?!

She stared at the innocuous wooden door as if it were the gates of hell, waiting to swallow her whole into fiery torment. She clutched the key card in her hand so tightly that it cut into her palm.

Melinda turned to run and then had the awful thought that she might hurt Pete's feelings if she did that. He was such a nice guy; the only person who'd been truly wonderful to her lately. He'd have danced with her. He'd come looking for her.

He wanted her. And Melinda wanted so badly to be wanted.

Oh, that's pathetic.

Really? There's a song about it. I want you to want me...

Forget it.

Mel turned around and marched three steps from the door. Then she heard the familiar *ding* of the elevator again, cheerful whistling, and Pete's hearty laugh.

"None of your business," he said to someone. "But yeah, you could say that. I've got a hot date waiting for me."

Aaaaaack!

Pete was about to walk this way, and she still had the Spanx on. She'd die before she'd let him see those.

Melinda sprinted for his room, as he stood chatting a little longer, evidently with a coworker here at the hotel.

She jammed the key card into the slot, fell inside and banged closed the door. She dived into the bathroom, eyeing his toiletries as she rucked up the skirt of her dress and yanked down on the waistbands of both pairs of Spanx. After a mighty tussle, she managed to roll both of them down her thighs at once, into a sort of microfiber pretzel, and then panicked.

She had no idea what to do with them. She shoved them into the trash can and wadded up some toilet paper to throw on top of them.

By the time Pete came through the door, she'd launched herself out of the bathroom and onto his bed, hyperventilating.

"Hello, beautiful," he said, grinning at her. He held a full bottle of champagne and two glasses.

"Hi," she huffed, leaning back on her elbows in what she hoped was a nonchalant pose. A drop of perspiration dribbled from her hairline down to her ear.

She took brief stock of the room—like hers, it was decorated in standard luxury-hotel fashion, with formal drapes at the sliding door to the balcony, and sheers in the middle for privacy. The bedspread was done in a fabric that coordinated with the drapes.

"What's got you so out of breath?" Pete set the champagne

down on a small, faux-Chippendale desk in the room, placed the glasses next to it and then began to work on the cork.

She cast about for an acceptable answer. The truth was completely out of the question. But so was, "I'm so desperate for you that I ran up seven flights of stairs, panting for your touch."

She swallowed. "Oh, you know…I was just warming myself up for you."

Pete knocked over the bottle. He licked his lips as he righted it. "Is that so?"

"Uh-huh. I got a little too warmed up, as a matter of fact."

The cork shot out of the champagne and hit the flat-screen television on the dresser. His hand shook as he poured the bubbly into one of the flutes, then the other. Then he walked over to the bed and stood over her, his eyes hooded, gazing down at her. Pete no longer looked like a teddy bear. He looked faintly predatory and all male.

"You're a naughty girl, Mel." He handed her one of the flutes.

She flushed and gulped some of the wine.

"In fact, you're just full of surprises. I had no idea."

He sat down on the bed next to her, depressing the mattress so that she rolled right into him. He leaned forward, his face close to hers, their lips almost touching. "You didn't come without me, did you?" His voice had gone husky.

Heat streaked like lightning to the core of her. "No…"

"I'm glad to hear that. I'd just have to make you come all over again." Pete touched his lips to hers and she felt another flash of electricity shoot through her, leaving traces along her erogenous zones.

He smelled spicy, enticing. The outdoorsy aftershave mingled with the scent of his freshly laundered shirt and a musky smell that was all Pete—which went to her head most of all.

He slipped his tongue into her mouth, touching hers, and

deepened the kiss. He tasted of champagne and mint and…
cocktail sauce? She wasn't sure, but then he set down his glass
and took hers away, too, and it didn't matter.

He took her face between his big hands and kissed her
with urgency. She couldn't think—she was all sensation, all
pleasure.

Pete's fingers threaded through her hair and he pushed
her back onto the mattress. He found the hidden side zipper
of her dress and pulled it down, down, down. He eased the
spaghetti straps off her arms and peeled back the bodice. She
wore a lacy black bra, strapless.

Pete kissed her cleavage and then freed her from the lace,
the tiny sand dollar from the beach rolling onto the bedspread. His face became a study in boyish awe. Speechless,
he mounded her breasts in his hands and then whistled like
a construction worker.

Mel laughed, glad not to have disappointed him.

"They're incredible…stunning." He simply stared at them
as if he couldn't believe what he was seeing.

"Yours to play with," she said, trying to catch her breath—
a lost cause. "For now."

Pete fumbled with the buttons on his shirt and removed it,
never tearing his eyes away from her body.

It was her turn to stare at his, to take in the solid mass
of furred muscle that was his chest, the gym-hardened, cut
arms, the tanned expanse of his skin. Her mouth went dry.

How could she ever have thought of him as a teddy bear?
Simple: she hadn't seen him shirtless in years.

And dear God, now he'd kicked off his shoes, peeled off
his socks and dropped his pants. Pete had the tough, built legs
of a soccer or rugby player. How could she have known? She
couldn't remember the last time she'd seen him in shorts. And
she'd never seen him in plain blue boxers, as he was now.

He moved towards her with an expression of ownership

that she'd never seen, either, a possessive gaze that made something inside her go all girly.

He mounted the bed and straddled her, then bent his head and kissed her again, the hair on his chest brushing her breasts erotically. He thrust his tongue into her mouth, the act imitating what he wanted to do between her legs.

When she was breathless, he turned once again to her breasts. He squeezed them together and took the peaks into his mouth, like a kid trying to devour two ice-cream cones at once.

Pure, hot pleasure overwhelmed her and reminded her that he was no kid. It surged between her legs and dampened her inner thighs. It spiraled through her belly, tugging at her womb.

Pete sucked harder, abrading her nipples with his tongue. Her powerful response to him came from somewhere primal; somewhere no other man had accessed before. A low scream tore out of her throat, shocking her, and turned to a keening noise as he continued.

She briefly considered shame, and rejected it. She threaded her fingers through his dark curls and pulled on them, her legs moving restlessly.

Pete tore his mouth from her breasts, rolled to the side and pushed the skirt of her dress up, over her knees and then above her thighs. Shame came rushing back, cresting as he gazed down at her, pooling at her core. She knew her thighs weren't slender.

But he didn't seem at all interested in evaluating the circumference of her thighs. Pete relieved her of her black lace thong before she could even squeak out a protest, and when she tried to pull down her skirt again, he grabbed her wrists. With one hand, he pinned them on the mattress, over her head.

"Let me look, Mel. I think you're gorgeous."

Heat rose in her cheeks and she muttered a denial.

"Gorgeous," he repeated. He released her wrists, eased off her dress and looked his fill while she lay naked and blushing. After a few moments, her discomfort had her rolling to the other side of the bed, where she swung her legs off the mattress and put her feet on the floor.

"Where do you think you're going, honey?" His voice was soft, but commanding. "And why?"

She struggled to verbalize her self-consciousness. "I—"

"Have you changed your mind?" He rounded the bed and took her chin in one hand. She could feel the heat of his body; smell his desire.

As she raised her gaze from the floor, she couldn't help but notice that he'd ditched his boxers. That part of Pete that she'd never dreamed she'd see…it was heavy, thick, hard. She remembered from the beach exactly what it felt like in her hand. How would it feel inside her?

The thought made her go weak.

"Have you changed your mind?" Pete asked, again. "It's okay if you have."

She moistened her lips with her tongue, still staring at his cock, knowing that her body was more than ready for him.

He forced her chin up, gently, but she wouldn't meet his eyes. Her pulse beat triple time.

"If you haven't changed your mind," he said softly, "then I want you to do something for me. I want you to lie back right now, on the bed, and spread your legs. Open your thighs, like the dirty girl you were pretending to be…open them all the way, until I can see pink."

Shocked, her gaze flew to meet his, but she looked away just as fast. Her breathing had gone fast and shallow, her pulse haywire. Those lighting streaks were coming in clusters, assaulting her erogenous zones.

"Pink," he repeated. "I want to see you. I want to stroke

you. I want to taste you. And then I'm going to make love to you."

She thought she might come on the spot, just from his words.

"So what's it gonna be, Mel? Hmm?"

To hell with shame…

She followed instinct.

She lay down for him.

She spread her thighs.

4

MELINDA WAS LAID OUT like a banquet in front of him, and Pete shook his head, a little dazed by the sight. Was it the champagne or pure lust that fogged his brain?

He eased himself onto the bed, noting her self-conscious blush. "You're beautiful," he said softly. "Do you know that?"

Her blush only intensified. She moved a shoulder ever so slightly, saying nothing, but everything.

And it got to him. Pete's heart turned over. "We've got to do something about this," he said firmly. "Right now."

Mel shot him a puzzled glance and tried to close her legs, which didn't work well since Pete moved quickly to position himself between them. He sat back on his heels, then ran his hands from her knees up to her thighs, his thumbs tracing the sensitive flesh on either side of her mons.

She shivered as he caressed her lightly there; let out a soft gasp. She parted her lips; so did he, rubbing a little more firmly against the slickness and paying special attention to the small nub that he knew would bring her the most pleasure.

"You like that?" he asked, as she pushed against him unconsciously. Her eyes had fallen closed and her breathing hitched.

"Yes…"

"I like it, too. You know you're beautiful?"

Mel's mouth twisted; again, she made no comment, and again, it bothered him. He slipped a finger inside her while still stroking that little fold of flesh. Tight, hot, wet, welcoming: the crazy mystery of a woman, the innermost cave that drew a man.

A small moan escaped her, and he smiled, knowing he was bringing her pleasure. Pete came forward on his knees and bent his head to her breasts, taking one into his mouth while still working his magic between her legs.

Her body began to tremble in mounting tension as he sucked, and he took his hand from between her legs, placing it instead on her other breast. He didn't want her coming too early.

She made a sound of protest but quieted as he slid his cock against her, teasing and exploring. She tried to guide him inside her, but he took her hands away. "This is for you," he said. "I want this to be all about you."

There were dozens of questions in her eyes, but he ignored them. He kissed her, tasting the champagne on her lips along with something sweet that was pure Mel. He wanted more of it. He slid his tongue into her mouth to explore, and denied his body's insistence on doing the same further south.

He kept teasing her there, though, and moved his mouth to her nipples again, abrading them lightly, sucking until she wrapped her legs around him and whispered, "Please…"

He wasn't ready to indulge her yet. "Say this aloud, Mel. Say, 'I'm beautiful.' I want to hear you."

"Pete, come on," she muttered, the blush beginning to reappear.

"Come on, what? I want you to say it."

"I'm not saying that." She reached for his cock and wrapped her fingers around it.

Yeah, oh yeah, his body said.

"No, Mel, you can't have it yet," his mouth said.

Dumb ass, said his body.

"Tell me you're beautiful."

She let go of him and lay her head back on the pillow, clearly frustrated. "I'm not playing this game with you, Pete."

"It's not a game," he said, stung.

"I'm not trading cheesy affirmations for…for—"

"Cheesy affirmations? Melinda, I just wanted you to acknowledge something which happens to be true." He stared down at her.

"It's not true, and we both know it!" she snapped.

"Yeah, darlin'," it is. Clearly you haven't been looking in any mirrors lately."

"Spare me. Really. Spare me the bad lines, Mr. Customer Service." She sat up, clearly with the intent of getting out of bed.

Pete had never been naked, fully erect and this instantly angry before in his life. Maybe it was the years of smiling in the face of hotel-guest abuse, or maybe it was having his kindness thrown back into his face. Maybe it was this particular woman.

He grabbed her by the shoulders and pushed her back down on the mattress, ignoring the shock in her eyes as she struggled against him.

"Listen to me, Melinda. You can have a complex about your weight if you want to. You can be self-conscious and awkward—that's your choice. But what you cannot do is call me a liar. Understand?"

She just stared up at him, wide-eyed.

"Does this—" he gestured bitterly at his raging erection "—does this look like customer service to you?"

She opened her mouth but only a squeak came out.

"Well, does it?" he roared.

"No," she said in a small voice.

"Okay, then." He nodded. "Now, do you think I get this way around women I think are ugly?"

After a small hesitation, she shook her head.

"Then I think you owe me an apology." Pete released her and rolled off the bed, stalking to the window. How in the hell had this gone so wrong? He took stock of himself with vague surprise: rigid muscles, heavy breathing, big scowl. Who was this guy? It certainly wasn't Peter S. Dale, Senior Account Manager. How had he gotten this pissed off?

A pair of soft, warm arms slipped around him from behind. "I'm sorry, Pete," Melinda said. "I'm sorry."

He could feel those spectacular breasts up against his back, and her legs brushing his. Her hands moved from his stomach up to his chest, her fingers combing through the hair and then tracing his nipples, which hardened immediately under her touch.

He closed his eyes as she smoothed her way down his belly again, to the springy hair just south of it. And bit back a curse as she took his cock into her hands and worked her woman voodoo on it until he felt like he could smash through stone walls with the thing. He was so hard it hurt.

Before he knew it, Mel had dropped to her knees in front of him and taken it into her mouth. Nothing had ever felt so good...

He stood there for a moment, lost in the sensations of it. Warm and wet, her tongue sliding along him, her hand wrapped tightly at the base. Ahh.

But he wasn't going to let her apologize this way. He slid his hands over her head, tunneled his fingers into her hair, and destroyed what was left of her updo. Then he took her by the shoulders and pulled her gently to her feet. "Come here, Mel."

"Did I do something wrong?"

"No, honey. You do everything right." He kissed her, loving the way her hair now tumbled free around her shoulders. He palmed her breasts possessively.

And she kissed him back without hesitation. "Then why…"

"Because," Pete said, "I want to make love to you." He took her by the hand and led her to the bed again. "If that's all right by you."

She nodded shyly and sat down.

He went into the bathroom and got a condom from out of his toiletries kit. He ripped open the packet, took it out and she helped him roll it on, her touch a sweet kind of torture.

"Now, where were we?" Pete asked ruefully.

Mel scooted to the middle of the bed, lay down and opened her legs. "Right here?"

"Yeah, right about there." He winked at her. "And the view is to die for."

MEL'S PULSE SKITTERED crazily when he looked at her that way, as if she were truly some kind of knockout. But men just got excited in the face of the female anatomy, didn't they? A centerfold in the privacy of the bathroom would probably produce that same glazed expression.

Then Pete launched himself at her like some kind of animal, and she didn't have time to be cynical. Because…dear God…his face was between her legs and his mouth was right there, and his big hands cupped her bottom, and her heels were hanging over his broad shoulders.

His hands pushed her thighs even further apart to give him better access, and she thought she'd split in two.

The tension in every muscle built until her insides went molten and poured towards where his clever, teasing tongue was. She was barely aware of thrashing against him, her body trying to celebrate and escape simultaneously.

She heard herself scream, felt the rumble in his chest as

he chuckled in satisfaction, registered the exultation on his wet face, framed by her thighs.

Then he moved over her, slid himself into her a couple of inches, and closed his eyes at the evident pleasure of it. Maybe he was trying to hold himself back. He opened his eyes again as if to ask permission to be rough.

"Yes," she whispered.

He drove into her with such force that she could almost feel him in her throat, making a sound that could have expressed either ecstasy or pain. "Melinda," he said. "I'm sorry. I can't help it."

"It's okay…I like it."

He pulled out and drove in again, and a tension coiled low in her belly at the sweet friction of it. She clutched helplessly at his shoulders, his neck—he was slick with perspiration and need. He smelled of sweat and man and her own essence.

She met him stroke for stroke, echoing his rhythm. When he bent his head to her nipples again, the tension low in her gut grew almost unbearable and she begged for release.

Pete slid a hand between their bodies and found her clitoris with his thumb. He toyed with it, massaged it as he pumped into her…and again she came apart, lifting off the bed and locking herself against him.

Electrified, spasming around him, she felt him tense, curse, and explode inside her before falling exhausted to the mattress on top of her. "Now," he said raggedly, "will you please, for the love of God, just say it?"

It took her a moment to register what he was talking about. Then she laughed weakly. "I'm…I'm beautiful?"

"Damn straight," said Pete. "Not only that…you are one hot piece of ass."

Since he said it in a tone that was close to reverence, she didn't take offense. Instead, in a state of wonder, she reached out and stroked his damp chest, which was still heaving—and because of her. Her, pudgy Melinda Edgeworth.

"In fact," Pete continued, "I wish I could do you again right now. Instead, we're going to have to wait a little while."

Mel snuck a look at the digital clock on the bedside table. "Oh, my God! I have to get back downstairs."

"Why?" he asked. But he knew why. People would notice they were missing.

In fact, a peculiar expression formed on his face. One that she found hard to interpret. It wasn't exactly embarrassment. Nor was it fear. It was halfway between guilt and trepidation.

She narrowed her eyes at him. "Why are you looking like that?"

"Like what?" Pete wouldn't meet her gaze.

"Like…I don't know…" She couldn't quite put her finger on it. "As if…"

They both jumped as a heavy knock sounded on the door. "Pete? Pete, are you in there?"

"Shit!" he whispered. "Please don't tell me that's—"

"Mark," Melinda said, gulping.

He vaulted off the bed and pounced on her dress, then her panties. He threw them at her. Then her bra. "Get into the bathroom!"

Melinda ran.

5

PETE TORE AFTER HER and grabbed a towel, which he wrapped around his lower body. Then he sprang towards the bed again, yanking the spread up over the tangled, sweaty sheets. It reeked of sex in the room. He headed for the sliding glass doors, which he opened to the balcony.

"Pete!" yelled Mark. "Open the door. I know you're in there."

Shit—the first place Mark would check was the bathroom. Pete wrenched open the door, put a finger to his lips, and dragged the still half-naked Melinda out. She now wore her bra and panties, but hadn't made it back into her dress. He pointed silently to the balcony. She sprinted.

"Mark, what the hell, man?" he called. "Hang on a minute—I was about to get in the shower."

"Dale, open this door. I have a bad feeling about who's in there with you!"

Pete spied Mel's purse on the dresser, and her shoes near the bed. He scooped everything up and bundled it onto the balcony after her. Then he pulled closed the heavy drapes.

Casually, he strolled to the door and opened it, yawning. "Mark? To what do I owe this honor?"

Mark loomed over him in his tuxedo. His breath reeked of Scotch. "Where's my sister?"

Pete put on his best puzzled face. "Huh? Why? Where's your bride?"

"Changing into her going-away outfit. You know we're spending the night at the Ritz. Where's my sister?"

"Melinda? I have no idea. I took her a glass of champagne out on the beach, asked her to dance. We talked for a little while. Then she said she'd rather be alone."

Mark's eyes narrowed suspiciously. He eyed Pete's towel and pushed past him, scanning the room but finding nobody there.

Back in high school, some asshole on the basketball team, Barton something, had asked out Melinda and tried to feel her up. He'd complained about spending a bunch of dough on dinner and not getting to see her tits.

Mark had beat him to a pulp when he found out. Pete was pretty sure that Barton had carried home his torn-off arm, his nose and possibly his head. Or so the rumor went.

Since Mark was now a full foot taller and half again as wide as back then, Pete wasn't interested in true confessions. He valued his arms. He didn't need his nose kicked inside out. And kissing up to corporate clients would be a tad difficult without a head.

Pete aimed a convulsive smile at his friend. "Dude, you paranoid freak. Did you really think I was having some sex orgy up here with Melinda? Please."

"All I know is that she's missing." Mark poked his head into the bathroom. "And so are you."

"I'm not missing. I'm right here."

"It smells like sex in this room," Mark growled, sniffing the air like a bloodhound.

Pete produced an embarrassed, hangdog expression.

"Dude. There are channels on the television for single men. What can I say?"

"Nice. So you've been sitting up here jacking off? Is that why you missed the cutting of our cake?"

Pete dragged his hands over his face. "Mark. I was there for the ceremony, which is what counts. I made sure everything was perfect for the reception. As an account manager for a major hotel, how many times do you think I've seen wedding cake being cut? We do receptions here every weekend. I can only take so much bland white frosting."

Was that an outraged snort from the balcony? He hoped not.

Mark's head swiveled toward it. He turned to Pete, his eyes narrowing again. "That noise…" he said slowly. "You've got her outside!" In four strides, he was whipping open the drapes.

Son of a bitch! "Mark, I can explain—"

He stared. There was nothing there but the moonlight. Nothing below but sand, lit by lanterns, and dark sea. No scantily clad Melinda. Not a shoe, not a hairpin, not a sign of her anywhere.

"Do you feel stupid, now?" he asked Mark.

Because he sure did.

His buddy wouldn't give him an inch. He looked back into the room. "No, I don't. There's a sweating bottle of champagne on the desk, and two glasses on the nightstand, one with lipstick on it. This room reeks, and you're acting strange. If it's not my sister you've had in here, then who is it?"

Pete shrugged.

"Kylie. Kylie's been missing, too. Are you slipping it to my aunt?"

"Mark, there are a lot of women at the wedding, okay? Maybe I don't feel like kissing and telling."

"Are you saying that the woman is married?" Mark looked genuinely shocked.

"I'm not saying anything! Jeez, will you get out of my face and stop giving me the Spanish Inquisition? I'm a consenting adult, so is she—and that's really all you need to know, my friend. Now, get back to your bride before she thinks that you're screwing around on her."

Mark frowned. "I'm worried about Melinda. Mom said she went to her room with stomach issues, but she's not answering the door."

"I'm sure she's fine," Pete told him. "She may have taken something to knock herself out. Like Benadryl."

"Or maybe she's passed out. Mom said she was pretty sure she'd had a bottle of champagne by herself." Disapproval permeated Mark's voice.

"Well, there you go. She's sleeping it off."

"If she'd just trim down a little bit, she'd find a boyfriend with no problem."

Anger bubbled up inside Pete. "You guys need to ease up on her. I think she looks great just the way she is."

Mark snorted. "Well, ask her out on a date, then."

"I just might. How would you like that?"

The growl came back instantly, and Mark glared at him. "I wouldn't. In fact, I'd take you apart. I'd rip off your arm and beat you with the bloody stump. Then I'd rip off your head. I'd friggin' kill you…"

"Good to know," Pete said, nodding. "Good to know."

MELINDA'S KNEES WERE SCRAPED, and so were the undersides of her arms. That's what she got for playing monkey-girl and climbing from Pete's balcony to the one right next to it, heart in her throat as she straddled the wall between the two and clung to it and the railings. Thank God the occupants of the room hadn't been there.

She was now fully dressed except for her shoes. She'd even wriggled back into the much-despised Spanx, which she'd dug out of Pete's trash can so he wouldn't find them. Mel took in the view of Biscayne Bay below, with the shadowy silhouettes and brightly lit windows of other buildings in the background. Miami was just waking up for the evening, its residents languidly having a cafécito and anticipating the night ahead.

Mel herself was all *gringa:* she yawned, sleepy from the champagne, the lack of food, and the mind-blowing sex. But then she shrank back, fully awake, when she heard Mark prowling outside and Pete's voice saying to him, "Do you feel stupid, now?"

She sagged with relief. She'd made the right call in shimmying over to the next balcony, a plus-sized Spiderwoman in nothing but her bra and panties.

Mark was giving poor Pete the third degree in there, pointing out the champagne bottle, the glasses, the rumpled bed…really, he was way out of bounds. Pete was playing the wronged innocent, lying through his teeth for her. And here she was, a grown woman, skulking in the shadows so that her brother wouldn't know she'd had a fling at his wedding.

What was this, the Middle Ages? Mark was behaving like a caveman, and they, Pete and Mel, were allowing it.

Then again, Mark had always had a temper, a protective streak a mile wide, and a wicked right hook. She didn't want to see Pete hunting for his nose on the beach in the moonlight. She didn't want a rift between the two friends, either.

So she stood there, reveling in what Pete had said to her. *You are one hot piece of ass…*

Nobody had ever called her that before. She couldn't help grinning. And then, once her teeth were bared, she got kicked in them—again—as Mark's voice carried clearly through the night.

If she'd just trim down a little bit, she'd find a boyfriend with no problem.

Hurt and betrayal knocked the grin off her face. It fell eight stories to the dark beach below and buried itself in the sand.

It was one thing to absorb the hints and the glances of her mother and brother. It was another to hear the hurtful words spoken aloud, and to someone else, someone outside of the family. Someone who'd just seen her naked, for God's sake.

Melinda, still reeling, barely registered Pete's response.

You guys need to ease up on her. I think she looks great just the way she is.

But she did hear it. And he sounded sincere.

Part of her fell just a little bit in love with Pete Dale right then—a silly part of her, maybe. But Melinda could actually feel it unfurling, giving a tiny wave of joy deep down inside her.

It wasn't enough to block the hurt entirely, just a small distraction from it…but Mel wanted to kiss him. And then she wondered if that was pathetic.

She stood there, growing irrationally angry at her gratitude towards Pete, instead of focusing on her anger at Mark.

She waited, biding her time, until Pete came back out onto his balcony alone. "Melinda?" he called softly. "Mel, where are you?"

She hesitated. Maybe she should just jump off the damned balcony and run for the nearest convent, so she'd never have to see a man again in her lifetime. But convents had lots of rules, and she'd never been particularly obedient. Or chaste, she thought ruefully.

"Mel?" Pete called again.

"Right here." She leaned out, stretched her arm around the concrete wall dividing the balconies, and waved at him.

"Jesus," he said. "How did you get over there?"

"How do you think?"

"Wait there," he ordered. "I have a master key. I'll let you out the door and you can come back into my room."

"Thanks. I think I'd have to take off my dress again in order to make the climb back over."

Pete laughed. "I have no problem with you doing that."

"Pervert." Melinda waited until Pete, now clad in only a pair of snug Levi's jeans, entered the room and unlocked the door to the balcony, sliding it open for her.

"Madame," he said, stretching out a hand to help her inside.

Mel took his hand, then caught a glimpse of herself in the room's large mirror and grimaced. She might be dressed again, but she looked scary. Her eye makeup was smudged, her lipstick was smeared, she had beard burn around her mouth and her hair...yikes. In disbelief, she put up a hand to touch it, and Pete laughed.

"You have clearly been having all kinds of wild sex with some bastard who took advantage of you," he said.

"No, really?" Mel was still fixated on her horrifying hair. As a result of the salty sea air, the humidity, and the half can of hairspray the salon stylist had used, she resembled an alpaca dragged through an inkwell.

"Yup. And he'd be happy to continue taking advantage, by the way." Pete pulled her to him and tried to slip a hand up her skirt.

"Stop that!" She knocked his hand away and looked around at the belongings of the people staying in the room. Feminine clothing exploded out of a carry-on bag, and a man's computer case lay open in an armchair. "Let's get out of here. I feel really strange being in these people's room."

She also felt a little odd being face to chest again with a half-naked Pete. How could she ever have thought of him as a teddy bear? As they snuck out of the room, it seemed impossible. Her inner thighs burned as she walked, scraped raw by his beard bristle. Other things in that area tingled and stung, as well. He'd been so deliciously rough.

He opened the door and stuck his head into the hallway, peering right and then left. All was evidently clear, since he tugged her out behind him and then into his room again, where she felt trapped instead of relieved.

Pete was unbelievably, unexpectedly hot. He was hung like a bull and fantastic in bed. He was kind. He liked her naked. And he'd gone and done something funny to her heart by defending her to her brother.

Now he looked at her with amusement saturating those calm gray eyes of his; enjoying their little conspiracy and inviting her to share the joke on Mark.

All of this added up to exceptional danger. If she didn't get away from Peter S. Dale right this minute, she was afraid he'd break her heart—just like every other guy she'd ever known.

6

PETE DIDN'T KNOW what to think of Melinda at this point. In the space of a few hours, she'd gone from vulnerable woman to bold seductress, then from shy, self-conscious schoolgirl to passionate lover. And finally from remarkable gymnast—he didn't think he'd have the guts to climb from one balcony to another on an eighth story—to crazed coward.

She'd bolted from his room like a horse out of the gate at the Kentucky Derby. Whether she was mortified or petrified, he didn't know. Maybe somewhere in between the two. But she'd used his comb to attack her hair—without stellar results—and scrubbed at her smudged makeup with a washcloth.

Then she'd abruptly said, "Gotta go!" And one turn of the knob and slam of the door later, she'd vanished.

Pete shrugged it off and climbed into the shower, but he couldn't forget the sight of her face, flushed and beautiful, as he'd entered her…and he'd never, as long as he drew breath, forget those breasts.

He soaped up and rinsed off, bemused to find himself hard again as he toweled dry. He wanted to see her again, no matter how awkward things might get with Mark. He would see her again.

As he put his tuxedo pants back on, a second knock came at his door. What the…? It was Grand Central Station around here tonight. Mel must have forgotten something. Pete opened the door, ready to tease her, ready to kiss her again.

His boss stood there.

"Peter?"

"Mr. Reynaldo!" What in the hell was the man doing here on a Saturday night?

Rafael Reynaldo was in his late fifties, a man of impeccable grooming and great charm. He wore a French-blue tailored shirt and a charcoal-gray suit that complemented the salt-and-pepper of his hair and neat mustache. One of his dark eyebrows rose as he took in Pete's shirtless, barefoot state. "Are you not attending the Kirschoff/Edgeworth reception downstairs, Peter?"

"I—I—I can explain, sir. A guest knocked a cup of coffee down the front of my shirt, and…"

Reynaldo took in the rumpled bed, the champagne bottle and the two glasses, just as Mark had. "I see." Then he glanced at Pete's white tuxedo shirt, which lay on the floor next to the nightstand. The not-stained-with-coffee tuxedo shirt. And his nostrils flared as he undoubtedly caught the scent of sex.

"You do not need to lie to me, Peter," he said.

Fire burned its way up Pete's face. This was so definitely not the path to a vice presidency at Playa Bella, Inc. It was more the path to the unemployment office. "Sir, I'm sorry. I—I was…unexpectedly sidelined…and I'm on my way back downstairs right now."

"Was she pretty?" The ghost of a smirk played at the corner of Reynaldo's mouth.

Pete opened, then closed his own mouth. "Yes, very," he croaked at last.

"You practice safe sex, eh?" Now the smirk emerged full force.

Would the floor please open up and swallow him whole? Or could a lightning bolt strike him instantaneously? "Of, of course. The safest."

Reynaldo nodded. "Well, then. I do suggest a shirt and some shoes before you rejoin our guests."

"Right." Pete swallowed convulsively and tried to ignore the perspiration rolling from his neck down to the small of his back. "Ha, ha!"

"Ha, ha, ha!" Reynaldo squinted at him with friendly malice.

"So. Was there something that you needed, sir?"

"Yes, Peter. Respect. And a grain of intelligence, as well. There are security cameras in Playa Bella. And your key card is electronically trackable, you know. So I suggest that in the future, you are careful about when you engage in, shall we say…recreational activities."

Pete knew he'd screwed up, but did the guy have to keep rubbing his nose in the wet spot? He looked at the floor.

"Sir, I will point out that I am technically not working this evening—I am a guest at the reception—but would you like my resignation?" His stomach lurched. How the hell would he find another decent job in this economy?

Reynaldo snorted. "No, Peter, I would not. I have hired hundreds, if not thousands of staff over the years, and believe you me, my boy, I've seen much, much worse here in Miami." He winked. "Besides, you should be in the dirty movies with your slick moves, eh?"

The back of Pete's neck prickled, all the tiny hairs there rising. He scanned the room for some kind of hidden camera, but saw nothing. Still he felt like throwing up. Had Reynaldo or security somehow filmed him with Melinda? Horrible visions of the two of them airing on YouTube filled his mind.

And then grisly images of Mark, tearing him apart and feeding him his extremities.

Reynaldo's mocking laugh filled his ears. "I am joking. No, you were not on camera."

His knees weak, Pete let the air slowly out of his lungs.

"How do they say it on that TV show, Peter? That you have been 'punked'? Is that it?"

He produced a weak answering laugh. "Yes, that's what they say." He wiped his brow. "You got me, sir."

"Yes, Peter, I did." That mocking laugh came again. "You may have got some, but I got you. I learn the American slang, eh? Is good?"

Pete forced himself to chuckle and nod. After all, he couldn't exactly tell his boss to go to hell, now could he?

7

MELINDA TOOK THE service stairs down the three flights to her room, just to make sure she didn't run into anyone she knew. She made the mistake of touching her hair again, and it felt like insulation material rolled in tar.

What she wanted and needed was a nice, hot, relaxing bath—and possibly a lobotomy. That way she wouldn't obsess about Pete, her forwardness with him, whether or not he would call her, and whether or not she wanted him to.

She fumbled her key card out of her evening bag and soon she was inside her own hotel room. She kicked off her shoes, wriggled out of her dress and padded barefoot into the bathroom, where she plugged the drain of the tub and started the hot water. Playa Bella had thoughtfully provided shampoo, bath oil and conditioner to their guests, and she wished she had two of the little bottles of shampoo.

Within minutes, she was sprawled naked in a hot bath and soaking her head—a good thing. The half a can of spray in her hair went from being sticky when dry to being gooey and slimy when wet. Yuck. She sat up and dumped shampoo into her hand, then attacked her scalp. Once she'd rinsed and repeated, she began to feel better.

Mel drained the tub and refilled it with clean water. She

added the entire bottle of bath oil, then lay back again and relaxed, emptying her mind of all criticism, all business worries and all of her secret angst about never getting married, dying alone and being eaten by her little dog.

She was slipping peacefully into a warm, mellow, Zen state when someone knocked on her door.

"Melinda?" called her mother's voice.

Nooooooooooooooooooooooooooooo!

Mel prayed that she'd just go away. No such luck.

"Honey?"

"What?" she hollered rudely.

"Are you all right?"

I was before you came along to annoy me. Aloud, she said, "I'm fine, Mom."

"May I come in for a moment?"

"Just a minute." Her peace destroyed, Melinda got to her feet, stepped out of the tub, and wrapped herself in a terry robe. She sighed, belted it and swaddled her dripping hair in a towel. Then she went to the door and opened it.

Her aging Barbie of a mother stood there, clearly concerned. "How are you feeling?"

"Huh?" Melinda had forgotten the lie about stomach troubles she'd told. "Oh…I'm fine now, thank you. I took some antacids."

"Mark said he knocked on your door earlier but there was no answer."

"I was sleeping."

Jocelyn stood there awkwardly for a moment, as if she didn't know what to say. But that was impossible, because she was a social butterfly and in charge of one of the big Miami charity leagues. She always knew the right thing to say. "Well, I'm glad you're feeling better."

"Thanks."

"Sweetheart, we don't see much of you lately. Your father and I wish you'd come by the house more often."

Maybe I would, if you didn't constantly drop hints about my weight and serve me cucumber rounds and water with lemon in it. Mel sighed.

"I know you're busy, though." Her mother still stood uncomfortably near the door.

Melinda felt guilty, as usual. Her mother had the ability to make her feel either guilty or furious within two seconds flat. "Mom, what? What's on your mind? Come in and sit down."

Jocelyn brightened immediately at the invitation, and Mel told herself she should be nicer to her. She should have more respect.

"I noticed that Pete took you some champagne while you were out walking on the beach. Wasn't that nice?"

Uh-oh. "Yes, it was very sweet of him." *Did you also notice that I'd already swiped an entire bottle?* Mel braced herself for a lecture.

"He's grown into quite a good-looking boy. Man, I should say…although it sounds ridiculous when I realize that I've known him since he was twelve or thirteen years old." Jocelyn laughed, the sound genteel and controlled. Had her mother ever let loose with a wild donkey laugh? One of genuine amusement?

"Don't you think he's good-looking?" she pressed Mel.

"Sure, I guess. I hadn't really noticed." Oh, God. *Please, please, please don't tell me that my mother watched me put my hand in his pants!*

"Well, he seemed quite taken with you."

"No…I'm sure he was just being polite. He's Mr. Customer Service, Mom. He works here."

"He does have lovely manners, doesn't he?"

Mel squirmed, thinking of the things she'd just done naked with Pete.

"Doesn't he?" Jocelyn was eyeing her strangely.

"What? Oh. Yes. Great manners." Maybe he'd send her a thank-you note.

"I heard that he's no longer seeing his girlfriend, so he's single. How about that?"

Mel shrugged.

"You should make an effort to talk to him tomorrow at the wedding breakfast, Melinda. Did you avoid salt tonight? Did you bring a skirt in a dark color?"

"Mom, please…" Mel sat heavily on the bed and dragged her hands down her face.

"Single men with good career prospects don't grow on trees, honey. College is a few years behind you, and you don't belong to many organizations where you might meet—"

"Stop!"

"—someone to settle down with. You don't belong to a gym…"

Where I could grab guys, pin them to the floor and make them smell my sweaty armpits?

"…or a church…"

Where I could trip them on their way down the aisle to the offering plate?

"…or an online dating service…"

As if I have the time.

"Mom," Melinda begged, "please stop! You're being hurtful, okay?"

Her mother sat on the bed with her, of all things, and tried to take her hands in hers. Mel stuffed them in the pockets of the hotel robe and glared at her.

Jocelyn smoothed her blonde hair back from her face. "I'm not trying to hurt you. I'm trying to help you, sweetheart."

"Well, you're making me crazy instead!"

Her mother's eyebrows drew together. "Someone has to

say these things to you. And since I am your mother, I get the pleasure."

"It is a pleasure to you, isn't it?" Mel's voice had risen, but she couldn't help it.

"That's not true."

"I think it is. You just can't stand me not being a carbon copy of you. Has it ever occurred to you that maybe I want to meet someone who loves me for who I am, not what I look like? Has it ever—"

Jocelyn's expression was pitying. "That's a nice notion, honey, but it's a fairy tale."

"Is it? Let me ask you a question. Are you so insecure in Dad's love that you can't let yourself gain a single pound for fear that he might dump you?"

Her mother froze, shock like ice in her eyes. The color drained from her face and then her nostrils flared. "How dare you say that to me?"

Mel was shaking now, but she refused to back down. "How dare you say the things to me that you do?"

Jocelyn stood abruptly, and then walked to the door on her spindly legs. "You're impossible."

"*I'm* impossible?"

"You're also rude, ungrateful and disrespectful. And if you refuse to change your attitude and your weight, you'll stay single for the rest of your life."

The words knocked the breath from Melinda for a moment. Then a flash of rage ignited her temper, and that triggered her mouth. "Is that right? Well, it may just interest you, then, that *I've had sex tonight, with the very guy you wanted me to throw myself at!* And you know what? He didn't have any complaints about my body."

Her mother didn't look quite so elegant with her jaw dropped open. Melinda had a moment or two of great satisfaction before Jocelyn snapped it shut again.

"Of course he didn't complain," she said scornfully. "You were easy and available. I'll bet he told you that you were beautiful, didn't he? And you took your dress right off for him." She shook her head as she opened the door and stalked through it. "You let yourself be used, Melinda. And I thought I'd brought my daughter up better than that."

The words were pure cruelty, aimed with perfect precision, and they hit their mark. Mel crumpled to the floor as the door closed, her pain so acute that she couldn't even cry.

Her body trembled uncontrollably, and she wrapped her arms around herself in a vain attempt to calm down. But the taunts reverberated in her head.

I'll bet he told you that you were beautiful, didn't he? And you took your dress right off for him.

Her mother was a horrible woman sometimes. But she was also right. He had told her that. *Let me look, Mel. I think you're gorgeous.*

She writhed now in shame. And worse, despite the shame, his words still sent a sexual frisson through her. So did the memory of his fascination with her body…and his mouth.

Mel somehow found the strength to crawl into the bed and pull the covers over herself, bathrobe, hair towel and all. She wasn't going to move from this spot until checkout time tomorrow.

Because one thing was for sure: she would not attend the wedding breakfast. She'd never, ever see Pete again, not voluntarily, anyway.

FULLY DRESSED IN HIS tuxedo again within five minutes, Pete headed downstairs in record time. He slipped back into Ballroom C, where the reception was winding down now—Mark and Kendra had evidently left.

He made sure everyone who wanted a last drink got one before the bar closed, and saw to it that the tables all got bused. He poured some seriously inebriated guests into a couple of taxis, and even escorted Mark's slightly tipsy Aunt Mildred to her room on the third floor.

He shoveled some last late-night partiers into the Starlight Bar and Lounge, Playa Bella's own nightclub, and kept an eye out for Melinda, but didn't see her. The person he kept seeing instead was Melinda's and Mark's mother, Jocelyn. And for some reason she was glowering at him, though her husband Richard was just as affable as always.

Pete spent a few minutes with the bride's parents to make sure they were happy with everything and had no questions about the final bill. Then he walked over to say good-night to the Edgeworths.

He'd eaten countless oatmeal-raisin cookies in Jocelyn's kitchen as a kid, and she'd been very warm to him at the beginning of the evening, so he couldn't account for the arctic chill in her voice now, unless...

"Mark and Kendra looked so happy," he said, placing a hand on Jocelyn's shoulder. "Didn't they?"

"Yes." She sidestepped quickly, shrugging him off, while Richard didn't seem to notice.

Had Melinda told her mother what she and Pete had done? No...why would she have? It wasn't the kind of thing a girl discussed with her mom over coffee. Or was it?

"You and your staff here at the hotel did a fine job," said Richard genially. "Very nice party. Thank you."

Pete shrugged modestly. "Kendra and her mother planned it down to the last detail. So it was easy for us. But I'm glad you enjoyed yourselves."

"As did you," Jocelyn said acidly.

Pete froze. Then he lifted an eyebrow. "Yes, it was great to see everyone after all these years."

Melinda had definitely said something to her mother, damn it. But why? And how much had she told her? He could feel heat rising up his neck and into his face, for the second time that evening.

"How's the old neighborhood?" he asked, looking for a safe topic of conversation.

"Fine," Jocelyn said, avoiding his gaze and hunting for something in her purse.

"Oh, nothing much has changed, except for a few more burglar bars and alarms," Richard mused. "Crime's even crept into Coral Gables, you know. Some of the incidents are pretty brazen. Our neighbors the Sanchezs had their front door kicked down, clean off its hinges. But their alarm went off, so whoever it was skedaddled before any other harm was done."

Richard was that kind of harmless guy who'd use the term *skedaddled*. Pete wished there were more of them left in the world.

"D'you know the Sanchez family, Pete?"

He shook his head. "They must have moved in after I left for college."

"Mmm. That's right, you headed down to Texas and got yourself some southern manners along with that BA in business." Richard winked.

Jocelyn, who'd been applying powder to her nose, snapped shut her compact with a little more force than necessary. "He learned how to sweet-talk women, didn't you, Peter?"

O-kaaaay. Pete chuckled mildly. "Well, I don't know about that, Mrs. E. I haven't been all that lucky in the babe department lately."

She shot him the lipless smile of a cobra. "That's not what I hear."

Richard's eyebrows shot towards his hairline. "Jocelyn," he said in reproving tones.

Oh, hell. Did Melinda's father know, too? No, he just looked puzzled by his wife's hostility. Pete hoped that she wouldn't explain anything to him. He felt awkward enough as it was.

"So!" He clapped Richard on the shoulder. "Are you staying at Playa Bella tonight, or driving home?"

"We're driving home. But we'll see you bright and early at the wedding breakfast tomorrow." Jocelyn really had the cobra thing down: she managed to move her head forward and then back while making the barest shimmy with her shoulders. It shouldn't have been menacing, especially not on a five-four blonde, but it sent a clear warning signal down Pete's spine.

"Great," he said jovially. "You know we'll do it up right. Playa Bella is famous for our mimosas, and the French toast is unrivaled. Now, do you have your valet ticket? I'll walk you out."

"Ah. Very nice of you, Pete." Richard preempted his wife, who'd opened her mouth to refuse the offer. He fished around in his jacket pockets for the ticket.

Pete would have sworn he saw just the tip of a black, forked tongue flicker out of Jocelyn's mouth, and blinked. Had he gotten some bad fish?

"Here we are!" Richard produced the wayward valet ticket and handed it over. They all made their way out to the marble foyer. One of the doormen opened a fifteen-foot-high entrance door upon sight of them, and Pete cast a glance heavenward in thanks that he was about to escape from Melinda's mother.

They stepped out into the humid Miami night air, he dealt with the valet guys and then murmured a good-night. Within seconds he was breathing a sigh of relief back in the air-conditioning, practically hiding behind a giant, ornate floral arrangement in the lobby.

He took a step towards his room, and another. And then something jabbed him in the small of the back. It felt like a gun.

Pete spun around and discovered that he'd been held up by Jocelyn's long fingernail.

"I want to talk to you," she hissed. "Not now. Not at breakfast. Tuesday morning. Eleven o'clock."

"I, uh, believe I have an appointment scheduled then," Pete stammered.

"Then cancel it." And with that, Jocelyn coiled herself back out the door.

8

MELINDA WOKE BLEARILY to a gentle tapping on her hotel room door.

"Room Service," came a faint call.

She frowned, but got out of bed and pulled on a robe. "I didn't order anything," she said to the uniformed maid outside.

"Compliments of Mr. Dale." The tiny woman came in with a tray and set it down on the room's desk. "Coffee, cream and sugar."

Mel got a couple of dollars out of her purse to give to the woman, and stared at the tray once she'd left. Next to the beautifully folded, snowy-white napkin was a single red rose. And under the rose was a cream envelope.

She stared at the envelope suspiciously as she poured a cup of coffee and mixed cream and sugar into it before taking a grateful sip. She drank most of the coffee before she finally slid the note out and read it. In neat but bold lettering it said:

Dear Melinda,
Last night was incredible…a wonderful surprise to find
out that the little girl next door has grown up to be all

sexy woman. I can't wait to see you at breakfast. In the meantime, how about some coffee?
Pete

She picked up the rose and smelled it; inhaled the deep, sweet floral velvet of its petals. She read the note again. He did have nice manners—he'd been sweet and thoughtful without making her feel cheap.

She picked up the envelope to slide the note back into it, and something fell out onto the tray—the tiny, perfect sand dollar she'd found on the beach and tucked into her cleavage. Another unexpected touch.

Mel had planned to get her things together and go home, skipping the breakfast, but now she hesitated.

Slinking out of here like a dog with its tail between its legs smacked of shame, and she had absolutely nothing to be ashamed of.

Nothing.

She and Pete were two consenting adults and they'd known each other for a long time. So what if it had been a booty call? They happened all the time.

And while she really didn't want to see her mother, she refused to run away and by doing so, validate Jocelyn's hurtful comments. So she had another cup of Pete's complimentary coffee, then ratcheted up her chin and headed for the shower.

FORTY-FIVE MINUTES LATER, Melinda stepped out onto the bayfront terrace where Playa Bella had set up the wedding breakfast. She wore a navy sundress with white polka-dots, some freshwater pearls around her neck, and white kitten-heels. She'd left her hair down.

While the coffee had helped clear her head, she was definitely feeling the effects of too much champagne the night before. Still, she greeted Aunt Mildred with a smile and a kiss on the cheek, and then chatted with some of the other guests.

Kylie, Melinda and Mark's very young aunt—and

Melinda's good friend—looked even more hungover than she was. And somehow sheepish, with an angry edge.

"Hey, Kylie," Mel said, as she gave her a hug. Her aunt was only a couple of years older than she was, a tall, statuesque blonde. Mel would have been in awe of her model good-looks, but since she saw her practically every weekend in a scruffy plaid bathrobe, unshaven legs and mangy flip-flops, she hadn't been intimidated by her in years.

"Hi, honey." Kylie seemed distant and wary, and scanned the crowd like a secret service agent, her usually warm, hazel eyes narrowed and cold.

"Looking for someone?" Mel asked, scanning people herself for any sign of Pete.

"More like avoiding someone," Kylie said cryptically.

"Who?"

"A complete jerk."

Mel's eyebrows shot up. "I didn't know any had been invited, except for maybe my mother."

Kylie's lips twitched. "On the outs with Joss again? Sorry."

Mel grimaced. "Yeah. So who's got you so pissed off?"

"Nobody." Kylie might be all woman on the exterior, but emotionally she functioned more like a guy. She was a great listener, but shared only when forced to.

Hmm.

Hadn't Mark said Kylie had been gone from the reception, too? Had she hooked up with someone? It wasn't like her, if so. Mel would try grilling her, but not in front of all their relatives.

She once again searched the guests for Pete.

Most of the younger generation seemed to be missing in action and were probably still asleep. Mel didn't spot a single groomsman other than…there he was.

He was dressed in khaki pants and a polo shirt, his hair still damp from the shower. He was giving some instructions to the servers near the buffet, serious for a moment, then nodding and smiling, clapping the shoulder of a young guy dressed in the kitchen uniform of a white cotton jacket.

He must have sensed her gaze upon him, because he turned and smiled at her. Mel experienced a curious sensation. Her heart seemed to melt, like one of Dali's wet watches. It slid through her insides and puddled into her shoes.

It wasn't a comfortable feeling, not to mention that it left a large, aching cavity in her chest. She stretched her lips into some semblance of a smile as panic rose in her throat like bile.

Booty call. That's all it was, you stupid, stupid girl. You have no feelings for Pete and he has none for you. Got that?

She turned away from Cryptic Kylie. "I'll call you later, okay?"

Her aunt nodded.

Mel glimpsed her parents, and searched quickly for someone else to go and have a conversation with. She wasn't ready to face her mother.

Great-uncle Ernie was parked in his wheelchair by himself, enjoying a mimosa while his sparse white hair lifted in the breeze coming off the bay. He looked a little like Charlton Heston, if Heston would be caught dead in those huge, dorky, wraparound sunshades that fit over a normal pair of glasses.

Heston also probably wouldn't be caught dead in a melon-colored polyester jacket and plaid pants in tropical hues, but Great-uncle Ernie wore his colors with pride.

"Good morning, Uncle Ernie," Mel said, kissing his cheek. "How are you today?"

"Oh, fine, just fine, thank you, Melissa." He beamed up at her, and she didn't bother to correct him. She'd be Marilyn next, and then Madeline.

Oblivious, Ernie continued. "Thought I'd lost my teeth, but I found 'em. Can you believe it? I put my teeth in my glasses case—though they didn't fit too well—and my glasses in a cup with the denture-cleanser. Let me tell you, that stuff is great for washing lenses! Who knew?"

She laughed. "Did you have too much wine last night, Uncle Ernie?"

"I hope so." He frowned. "Can't say as I remember."

"Beautiful wedding, though, wasn't it?"

"Oh, yes…even if the bride did get the hiccups during the vows. Cute, really. Never seen that before. Have you?"

"No," Mel said honestly.

"Your brother must give her indigestion," remarked Uncle Ernie.

Melinda was still laughing at this when Pete appeared at her elbow with a mimosa in each hand. "Hello, Gorgeous. A little hair of the dog?"

"What dog?" asked Uncle Ernie. "Can't abide dogs in restaurants and hotels. Hated Paris. Ten dogs in every café, I tell you." He snorted. "*Est ce vous avez fleas dans votre cappucino?* Ha. I'd rather be in a nice Howard Johnson's any day, and get no fur in my food."

"Playa Bella doesn't allow dogs, sir." Pete's lips twitched, but otherwise he kept his face admirably composed. "That's quite an excellent French accent you have."

"You bet. I was hot for this little French gal I met at the health club—this was back in the days when I had functional knees and ankles, you know—and when she said she taught at the community college I signed up for frog lessons real quick. She wouldn't teach me any dirty words, though, and I figured out pretty quick that she was seeing some Cuban fellow." Uncle Ernie's mouth turned downward until another sip of his mimosa brightened him up.

Melinda met Pete's amused gaze over his head. She got lost in those rainwater-gray eyes of his, and forgot to be self-conscious.

"I like that dress," he said, as they edged away from old

Ernie. "It looks a lot more comfortable than the one you had on last night."

"It is," she said in heartfelt tones.

"Of course, I like what's under it a lot, too." He winked.

She felt the heat burning her cheeks. "About that, Pete—I'm, um, sorry that I…" Grabbed your dick like a drowning woman clutches at a piece of timber?

"Sorry about what?" he interrupted.

"Oh. Well. It's just that I had a lot to drink, and, um…"

"It was the champagne goggles, you mean? You'd never have touched me sober, ugly beast that I am?"

"What? No! No, that's not what I meant—" She stopped, flustered.

Pete's eyes twinkled. He was deliberately teasing her. "So, you didn't have nightmares about me? Horrible dreams in which you begged me to put my clothes back on?"

"No! I—"

"You're really cute when you blush, by the way."

What was she supposed to say to that? Thank you?

"But why are you blushing?" Pete looked perplexed.

"Because…I don't normally, um, unzip guys' pants—"

"Really? That's a damn shame." He sipped at his mimosa, eyeing her over the rim of the glass.

"…or grab their…"

"I didn't know it was possible for someone's skin to turn quite that red," Pete mused. "I think it might actually be dangerous."

"…parts," she finished desperately. Then she drank half her mimosa in a single gulp.

He touched his cold glass to her hot cheek, sending a shiver down her spine even in the humidity. "So what you're telling me is that my, er, part, was endowed with a powerful magnetic force that drew you helplessly towards my zipper. Mine was special. You couldn't help yourself." He winked again.

She stared at him, her mouth working. "No, what I'm saying is that I had too much to drink."

"Aww, and here I was beginning to be seriously flattered. Not to mention turned on again." Pete came a couple of steps closer, right into her personal space, and sucked all the oxygen out of it.

She could smell the soap he'd used that morning, and that clean, breezy aftershave. The quirk in his mouth was addictive. Her fingers itched to trace it.

Her heart hammering, Mel took a step back. "You don't have to flirt with me."

His eyebrows drew together. "What if I want to flirt with you, honey? What if I was going to ask you what you're doing this Saturday?"

Her heart leaped, and then fell again. He was just being polite about Saturday. She shrugged uncomfortably. "I mean, just because of last night, you shouldn't feel obligated to—I mean, I'm a big girl. I know it meant nothing."

He tilted his head and gazed down at her quizzically. "It meant something to me, Melinda."

"It was just sex," she blurted. "A booty call. I get that."

Pete opened his mouth to say something—probably a polite denial of what Mel knew to be true—but snapped it closed again as her mother and father appeared at her elbow.

"Melinda," said Jocelyn in frosty tones. She smiled brightly, though—too brightly.

"Hi, sweetheart," Richard said, kissing her cheek. His gaze darted from her mother's face to hers and then back again. Clearly, he knew there was trouble between them.

Pete looked actively uncomfortable, shifting from foot to foot, but produced a hearty grin.

"And Pete. How are you this morning?" Richard stuck out his hand. He and Pete shook.

"Peter, I noticed that one of the buffet trays is empty," her mother said coolly. "And that table in the corner? It's littered with dirty plates and utensils."

"Mom, Pete is not a waiter," Mel said through gritted teeth.

"No, but he does supervise the staff, don't you, Peter? When you're not busy, that is."

"Thank you for alerting me, Mrs. Edgeworth," Pete said smoothly. "I hope you'll excuse me while I take care of those issues. Enjoy your breakfast." And with those words, he vamoosed, leaving Mel with her parents.

"Richard, darling, would you get us some coffee?" Jocelyn asked, never taking her gaze from Melinda's face.

Mel raised her chin and squared her feet, bracing herself for whatever came next.

"Drinking again, Melinda?" Her mother gestured to her mimosa.

Mel's hand clenched around the glass. "What do you mean, again?"

"Didn't you have enough last night?"

"No, Mother. Clearly I didn't."

Jocelyn shrugged. "Empty calories."

Melinda raised her flute and drained the contents, barely restraining the childish urge to wipe her mouth with the back of her hand and then belch. "They're well worth it to me."

"Melinda, I think you owe me an apology."

She gasped. "You think I owe you one? It's the other way around."

"You owe me respect, young lady."

Mel took a deep breath. "Respect is a two-way street, Mother. If you'd respect me enough to stop needling me about my weight—"

"The only reason I do that is because I care about you! And I'd like your life to be different."

"Yeah? Well, it's my life! So you can stop caring. Because if this is the way you demonstrate motherly love, then I'm terrified to see what you do to people you hate." Melinda whirled around to leave and slammed headlong into her father, who'd arrived with two cups of coffee for them.

The cup with cream went all over her dress. The black coffee soaked her dad's shirt. Not a drop spilled on her perfect mother, of course.

"Dad, I'm so sorry! I was trying to get away from her—" Mel shot a glance at Jocelyn, who turned her back and ignored her.

A waiter came to the rescue with a couple of cloth napkins, and they mopped miserably at themselves.

"What is going on between you and your mother, Melinda?" Her father spoke under his breath, and his tone was gentle, but he was clearly frustrated.

"Ask her! I'm tired of being treated like a criminal if I eat something with more than a hundred calories in it. I'm tired of being told I'll never catch a man. I can't stand being around her—she's a walking reproach and clearly I'm nothing but an embarrassment and a disappointment to her!"

Richard sighed. "That's not true. Your mother loves you, Mel."

"She has a funny way of showing it."

"And we're both very proud of you."

Melinda stood on tiptoe to kiss him on the cheek, inhaling the familiar scent of Old Spice and cigar smoke that characterized her father. "Thank you. Now, I'm sorry but I have to go. I can't be around her right now. I hope you understand."

Richard nodded unhappily. "I do."

She turned and started to walk away. She'd only taken a few steps when he called, "Melinda? Do you need any cash?"

She stopped. She looked over her shoulder at him and shook her head. "Thanks, Dad. But no." *I'm a grown woman with a business and I no longer need movie money.* "It's very sweet of you to offer, though."

Mel made her excuses, retrieved her belongings from her room and checked out of Playa Bella. She never once ran into Pete.

It was just as well. He wasn't going to call her, anyway.

9

ON MONDAY, PETE WAS still disappointed. Melinda had disappeared without saying goodbye, and he'd never had a chance to get her number. Fortunately, her business number was easy to locate.

He sat, lost in thought at his desk, picturing her at the breakfast as she stumbled through her apology for unzipping his pants. He'd loved that she did that. He remembered the unexpected surprise, the delicious shock as her warm little hand had slipped inside the fly of his boxers and taken him in a firm grip. Had stroked him until he thought he'd blow right there on the beach.

And she'd felt the need to apologize?

She'd felt the need to tell him that she understood that it meant nothing; that it had just been a booty call?

Pete frowned. He hadn't thought beyond the instant attraction he felt for her, beyond the heat of the moment. He'd just acted. And now she was complicating things by stating baldly how uncomplicated they were. Damn it.

It was her vulnerability that got to him. The way her mouth had trembled ever so slightly as she said it. He'd instantly wanted to reassure her; to do exactly what she was telling him he didn't have to do.

Did that make him ornery? No. It just meant that he liked her. He wanted to make her feel good.

There'd been something brave in the way she faced up to the "fact" that things would end in a one-night stand. Something dignified and sad about the way she'd let him off the hook. And that something, whatever it was, touched a chord within him. The fact that she had low expectations made him want to raise them.

Pete pulled up the internet on his computer and found her business number. He was about to dial her when Mr. Reynaldo walked into his office. He silently thanked God that he hadn't been caught making a call to a woman after the fiasco over the weekend.

"Buenos dias, Pedro," said his boss.

"Buenos," Pete said, grinning his trademark customer-service grin, even though he hated it when his boss called him Pedro. "How are you, Mr. Reynaldo?"

"After looking over the books, I am very well, thank you. You may entertain as many ladies on the job as you wish, as long as you continue to increase my revenue."

"Uhhh." Pete fumbled for the appropriate response, while wanting to point out that he really hadn't been "on the job" when "entertaining" Melinda. "That…isn't something I… make a habit of, sir."

His boss waved a hand dismissively. "You spoke to me about the vice president of development job a couple of months ago."

"Yes." One of the reasons Pete had taken the job at Playa Bella was its vast upward potential. If he pleased a man like Reynaldo, a man with unlimited capital and a voracious appetite for expansion, he could write his own ticket.

He wouldn't be like his dad, trapped for years in some stodgy, compartmentalized corporate behemoth, being micromanaged and going gray while he waited for three percent annual raises. Pete was convinced it had made his old man crazy. And violent, when he drank.

Pete had no intention of becoming like him. He'd deliberately become his polar opposite.

Reynaldo took a moment to examine his manicure, turning his buffed nails this way and that under the light. "The job," he said, "is yours—if you bring new business up another twenty percent by year's end."

Pete was elated, even as he realized this was a tall order. He'd have to hustle, wheel and deal, and schmooze in his sleep to achieve the goal, which was, when he broke down the numbers mentally, to bring in almost a million dollars worth of business.

"Thank you, sir," he said.

"Don't thank me yet, Pedro. But make it happen, and you may keep a naked hooker in your office at all times, eh?" Reynaldo winked at him. "I'll even put her on the house."

Pete forced himself to laugh, though he was secretly appalled. "That's…not necessary, sir."

"I am simply trying to tell you, señor, that I do not much care what you do as long as you make me sufficient money. *Comprendes?*"

Pete nodded.

"Good. We understand each other. Now, what are you doing this Saturday night?"

He'd mentioned Saturday to Melinda, but Pete said casually, "Nothing important. Why?"

"I want you to come to a fundraiser for Governor Vargas and meet his campaign manager. They will be organizing many more political events, you see. We'd like several of those events—"

"To take place at Reynaldo hotels," Pete finished. "I get the picture."

"So. By the end of the evening, you will be the campaign

manager's best friend, eh? If he golfs, you golf. If he fishes, you fish. If he pays a dominatrix to humiliate him, you, too, like to be spanked and told you are a very bad boy."

Pete sighed inwardly. Aloud, he said, "I refuse to wear a black leather harness or put one of those rubber balls in my mouth, sir." He laughed.

Reynaldo did not. "You refuse nothing, Pete. *Comprendes?* He wants three transvestite pygmies and the original Bat-mobile, you procure."

Pete didn't like the sound of that much, but he doubted strongly that the guy would be that weird. He just hoped he didn't have to find illegal drugs for him. He didn't want any part of that.

"So. I will pick you up here at Playa Bella at 7:00 p.m. on Saturday."

"Yes, sir."

Reynaldo strolled out of the office with the sinuous grace of a jungle cat. Pete was beginning to wonder if he could trust him as much as one—especially when it was hungry. The longer he worked for Reynaldo, the less he cared for the man.

MELINDA GAVE A SIGH of relief to be back behind the scenes of her bakery, where she belonged, and not on display in Kendra and Mark's wedding. She'd calmed down after a heart-to-heart about her mother with Kylie. As Jocelyn's adored younger sister, Kylie loved her. But she also knew her faults and was able to put them into perspective in a way that Mel just couldn't.

Kylie knew her secret now—though Mel still didn't know Kylie's. She'd brushed off questions and changed the subject. Mel had finally given up, but she had an instinct that Kylie had something going on with, of all people, Dev. A banker and an ex-rocker? She couldn't imagine two people less suited to one another...

Mel gave up her speculating and turned her attention to her shop. The cool, stainless-steel appliances of her commercial kitchen soothed her as nothing else could, and the scent of the finest ingredients money could buy permeated the air.

She cut no corners; used nothing fake or full of fillers or chemicals. No commercially produced, boxed pudding mix; no lab-mixed chocolate substitute; and above all, no canned, aerosol-sprayed Insta-Wip "cream" insulted her customers. They got the real deal, the purest taste, calories and all.

Her mother had once requested that Mel make a cake using sugar-substitute, fake egg whites and zero-calorie Insta-Wip. Mel suggested that she glue a bunch of Twinkies together instead and tie a bow around them. And that had been the end of that discussion.

The sight of Mel's bulging order book now galvanized her, though in all honesty she'd be hard-pressed to make the rent without Franco Gutierrez's Java Joe's order.

Mel closed her eyes, wondering if she could have handled him differently. Could she have laughed it off? No. Maybe a pinch on the rear could be brushed aside, but the man had stuck his beefy hand down her panties. There was simply no going back from there—especially not when he'd suggested, in a very nasty way, that she should be nicer to him if she wanted to keep his account.

Even her Inner Drill Sergeant couldn't fault her reaction. He simply cleared his throat and growled that she had to work harder to replace the lost income. And she'd have to buy more of her supplies using credit. The thought made her feel slightly ill, and she slid open the bakery case to heist an oversize chocolate-chip cookie. It would settle her stomach.

Don't eat that! snapped the sergeant. *It's four-hundred calories at a minimum.*

Mel crunched down on it and hoped what she swallowed would hit him in the face.

Her assistant, Scottie Duval, waved at her and then continued his task of checking in inventory from a chocolate supplier in Belgium. Scottie resembled a very fashion-conscious leprechaun, with his red hair, narrow chin, wickedly slanting pale eyebrows and pointed ears that always managed to poke through his latest 'do.

He spritzed his face regularly with lavender water mixed with a little moisturizer to combat the drying effects of the air-conditioning. And he complained that the white cotton uniform she made him wear washed him out and made him look pasty.

Scottie was a genius with marzipan, though—he could sculpt anything a customer could conceive of—and he could roll fondant smoother than a baby's behind.

Just as important, he loved Mami, and not only kept her when Mel needed him to, but competed with Mel to make the tastiest dog cookies from scratch.

"I'm going to win today," he informed her with a smirk. "Liver snaps flavored with a touch of fontina."

"Nope." Mel set her hands on her hips. "Because I made her favorites—sweet potato and whitefish biscuits."

Scottie's eyes narrowed and he pursed his lips. "We'll just see about that, missy. We'll put them side by side and see which one she goes for."

"Fine."

Scottie kept his "Mami-Munchies" in a pale blue tin, studded with pink French poodles being walked by fashionable ladies. He reached for the tin and took out a liver snap. Of course he'd used a daisy-shaped cookie cutter, and iced them with yellow and pink frosting. Show-off.

Mel went to her own jar of treats and took out a fat biscuit. She'd used a fish-shaped cookie-cutter and iced hers in ocean blue and turquoise frosting. She'd also added silver "eyes" and cute little red smiles.

Together, they marched back to her office and opened the door. Mami really wasn't supposed to be on the premises— the health department would freak—but Mel reasoned that as long as she kept her in the office and she had no access to the kitchen, what the health department didn't know wouldn't hurt them. Mami got a bath every Sunday and went to the groomer's regularly, after all.

The little dog leaped up from her pink-velour beanbag and trotted over eagerly, eyes bright. Her tongue—the same shade as the beanbag—lolled out of her mouth. She weighed maybe nine pounds, if that.

"Hi, sweet girl!" Melinda said.

"Baby want a cookie?" Scottie crooned, crouching down with his butt in the air.

At the mere mention of the word "cookie," Mami began to spin around in circles.

"Biscuits are better, aren't they, sweet girl? Hmm?" Mel dangled the fish-shaped treat a couple of feet from the dog's nose, and she stood up on her hind legs.

"Cookie, cookie, cookie!" Scottie said, waving his daisy.

Mami looked from one to the other and yipped.

"Sweet potato and whitefish is your yummy-yummy favorite, isn't it, Mami?" Mel's voice had degenerated into blatant baby talk.

"Liver and fontina…fit for a princess puppy! There's no resisting, darling. Come over to the Dark Side."

"Okay," said Mel. "On the count of three, we put them down and see which one she goes for first."

"Loser has to deal with Mrs. Temperley when she comes to pick up her husband's birthday cake."

"Fine. Don't let me down, Mami," Melinda muttered.

Two wary combatants, they squared off.

"Ready?" Mel bent at the waist, one hand braced against her knee, the other one holding her fish biscuit.

Scottie nodded, poised to spring forward with his cookie. Mami yipped again, as if to say, "Let's get on with it!"

"One," Mel said. They both bent forward even more. "Two. Three!"

They each slapped their treats on the floor, right in front of Mami's tiny nose, which worked almost comically, twitching back and forth as she sniffed first the daisy cookie, then the fish biscuit. She cocked her head and sniffed at the daisy again.

Melinda was mortified when she daintily took it between her teeth and crunched down.

"Yes!" shouted Scottie. "I knew you were a lady of discriminating tastes, Princess!"

Mel glared at him.

Scottie gloated. "I guess she has a new favorite cookie."

"Huh." Melinda was only partly mollified when Mami eagerly chowed down her fish biscuit as well, and then looked around for more.

"Traitors don't get seconds," Mel said, scratching her behind the ears. Mami wagged her tail, not understanding a word. When Mel failed to give her more cookies, she tried spinning around in circles again.

"Go ask your best buddy, there."

Scottie preened. "That would be *moi,* baby girl." Mami ran to him, tiny tail wagging. He scooped her up.

"Cookie slut," Mel murmured, and picked up the order book. Not that she herself hadn't been a slut just a couple of nights ago… She wondered if Pete did actually want to see her on Saturday night. Then her mother's words echoed in her mind again, try as she might to banish them.

You were easy and available. I'll bet he told you that you were beautiful, didn't he? And you took your dress right off for him.

Even two days later, humiliation and uninvited suspicion

heated her cheeks and caused something inside her to physically ache.

Scottie finally gave back Mami, who snuggled into Mel's chest and poked her little nose under her arm. Then she pulled it out again and looked up at her with adoring brown eyes.

Mel's heart melted. She rained kisses all over Mami's fuzzy head. Then her competitive instincts kicked in and she headed for the computer to do a search. Liver and fontina? She'd do Scottie's recipe one better: she'd add bacon. And maybe even some gouda, just to show him who was truly boss.

10

TUESDAY MORNING ARRIVED despite Pete's best efforts to will it away. And the hands of his clock spun all too quickly toward eleven, when he'd have the dubious pleasure of Jocelyn Edgeworth's company once again.

He really couldn't imagine what she had to say to him, or what he would say in response. It wasn't the eighteenth century, so she couldn't possibly be about to demand that he make an honest woman out of her daughter after despoiling her.

He supposed that she would demand that he not see Melinda again, which he wasn't at all prepared to promise. He genuinely liked Mel, and decided that neither his friendship with her brother nor attempted bullying by her mother would dictate his next move, complicated as the situation might be.

Pete braced himself for a difficult conversation. He searched for ways to be tactful.

"Mrs. Edgeworth," he'd say, "I understand your concern for your daughter's happiness and your desire to protect her from hurt. But I can't promise not to see her again, and I hope you will understand and forgive that. She's an adult, and so am I."

Jocelyn would simply have to accept his position gracefully, in the face of his calm, polite demeanor.

When she did, in fact, sweep into his office dressed impeccably in a beige linen pantsuit, pearls and heels, he was ready for her. "Mrs. Edgeworth," he said, standing and extending his hand. "How nice to see you again. To what do I owe the honor?"

She lifted a perfectly groomed eyebrow at him and sat down in his visitor's chair without being invited. "I'm here with a business proposition for you, Peter."

It was his turn to raise his eyebrows. This was unexpected, to say the least. "A business proposition?"

She nodded. "May I be blunt?"

"I certainly can't think of a way to stop you," Pete said with a disarming smile. "So, please. Speak your mind."

"You slept with my daughter."

"Uh…"

"Don't bother denying it. She told me."

Pete knew this, though he was still puzzled as to why Mel had said anything, and his expression must have reflected it.

"I was," she said dryly, "encouraging her to look at your… shall we say…eligibility."

Now he was really confused. "You were?"

She nodded. She looked down at her clasped hands, unclasped them and began to toy with her wedding ring. "Melinda is very dear to us."

"That's understandable. She's your only daughter." *Here it comes. The demand that I stay away from her. Eligible or not.* He couldn't believe that anyone still used the word.

"I'm not very good at—" Jocelyn broke off. "That is to say—" She frowned, looking severely annoyed. She took a deep breath.

Pete waited.

"I seem to hurt my daughter without even trying," she said at last. "Without even opening my mouth, at times."

Pete couldn't think of an appropriate response. He re-

mained silent and stretched out a hand to make an infini-
tesimal adjustment to the stance of the bronze Longhorn on
his desk.

He couldn't imagine what any of this had to do with him.

"I think Melinda's life would be very different if she were
to lose, say, thirty pounds."

Pete lifted his eyes from the Longhorn. "She looks great
the way she is," he said.

"Oh, Peter, stop being so polite."

"I'm not—"

Jocelyn waved a dismissive hand. "Peter, what is your objective here at Playa Bella?"

"Pardon?" He was bewildered at the sudden change in
subject.

"What is your objective as senior account manager here
at this hotel?"

"To make money, ma'am. To bring in more business."

She nodded sagely. "I guessed as much. And what happens if you do that?"

"I…uh…well, I get promoted."

"Excellent. Well. That brings me to my business propo-
sition. As you know, Peter, I'm on the boards of the Have a
Heart Foundation, the Fresh Air Foundation for Lung Cancer
Awareness, the Muscular Dystrophy Foundation, the Junior
League and others. Every year we look for venues for our
charity balls and other fundraisers like our Holiday Bazaar."

"Okay." Pete raised his eyebrows quizzically.

"I am prepared to steer business—a lot of business—to
Playa Bella, if you will do one simple thing for me."

Oh, here it comes. "And what would that be, ma'am?"

"I want you to continue seeing my daughter."

Pete gaped at her like a guppy.

"Melinda has very low self-esteem. I may have contributed
to that, and I'd like to help her…blossom. Grow into herself."

Pete continued to stare at her, flabbergasted. "Ma'am, I can't—"

Jocelyn raised a hand. "Hear me out. You saw an easy target in Melinda, did you not?"

"What?"

"She's a bit zaftig. Plump. Not used to a lot of attention from men. Yet you told her she was beautiful, or something along those lines, and she lay down for you—"

"No! Is that what Mel told you?"

"Not in so many words."

"Well, I'm sorry, but it's not true," Pete said, outraged.

"Isn't it?"

He cast back in his memory. Sure, he'd complimented her. How was that a crime? How was that manipulating her into bed? He hadn't. The truth—that Mel had unzipped his pants and grabbed a good handful—he would die before sharing with her mother. He wouldn't for the world humiliate Melinda that way. There were some things that mothers simply did not need to know.

"Regardless," Jocelyn said imperiously. "What happened at the wedding reception isn't really my concern. It's what happens next. Melinda will be crushed if you don't call her, and you weren't planning to, were you?"

"Yes, I was going to call her, as a matter of fact!"

Jocelyn lifted her eyes heavenward. "Of course you were, Peter. Of course you were. And now you'll be sure to do so, hmm? Because I can bring you hundreds of thousands of dollars worth of business."

Pete felt his blood pressure rising to dangerous levels. Never in his life before had he felt the urge to punch a woman.

"And you'll get that promotion," she continued. "And Melinda will gain some self-esteem, and I'll feel as if I've done something to make things up to her. And everything will be rosy." She smiled.

"I will be calling her, Mrs. Edgeworth," Pete said, "but not because you've asked me to and not because you're offering me this bizarre 'business proposition' of yours. Are we clear?"

She gave him her cobra smile. "You don't have to admit it to yourself, Peter, if it makes you uncomfortable. Few human beings can acknowledge their true motives for doing things. Tell yourself whatever you need to, darling."

She was truly chilling. Pete marveled at her.

She stood up and slid the handle of her Chanel bag over her arm. "Now. Of course I'm not asking you to marry her. You'll have to let her down easy at some point."

"Oh?" Pete said, struggling to keep a lid on his temper. "And how do you suggest that I do that, since you've got this all planned out?"

"Peter," she said with heavy tolerance. "I'm not a monster, after all…"

Yes, you are.

"…that's up to you. You're an innately kind human being—"

Which is more than you are!

"—I do credit you with that—so I trust you to do things gently and humanely."

"Well, aren't you a peach." He was sorely tempted to pick her up bodily and throw her out of his office. Had he really eaten this woman's oatmeal-raisin cookies as a child? Had he really never seen this side of her? No wonder Richard's posture always looked stooped, his expression faintly browbeaten and vague, as if he lived in an alternate reality.

"I realize that you're angry with me right now, Peter. But do think it over. And if, as you claim, you were going to call my daughter anyway, then what do you have to lose? You can keep your integrity and make lots of money for your hotel at the same time." She produced her bloodless smile again.

"I can tell you're itching to say no. To defend your honor. To throw me out. Aren't you?"

Pete took a deep breath, his jaw tight, and said absolutely nothing. He didn't trust himself to be polite, and that unnerved him. He was always polite. He never lost his temper—that was his father's domain, and Pete had sworn he'd never go there, would never be like him.

She shook her head, still smiling. "All right, then. Let me put it this way. If you can't do it for yourself—if you can't do it for me—then do it for Melinda. Because you and I both know that she deserves better than a one-night stand."

The witch! Pete felt his mouth drop open again. How had she managed to turn the tables on him so neatly? How had she set him up to look like a bad guy if he refused her unethical offer?

Jocelyn Edgeworth patted his shoulder and he recoiled from her touch. Then she turned on her heel, blew him a kiss and walked out of his office with his balls in her designer pocketbook. Damn the woman! Was there any way out of this dilemma?

"No, Mrs. Temperley," Melinda said patiently, "I can't really change the message on your cake at this stage."

"Why not?" Mrs. T. was in her early sixties, but looked no more than fifty thanks to a gifted surgeon, a strict yoga regimen and a blissful disregard for anyone but herself.

"Because the fondant is dry and so is the butter-cream we used for the letters."

"Can't you pick them off and start over?"

"No, I'm afraid I can't do that without ruining the cake."

Mrs. Temperley's botoxed lips turned down at the corners. "But I wrote a poem for Stan, and I want it inscribed on his cake."

"Can you recite the poem instead as you give him the cake?"

Mrs. T shook her head.

"Then how about writing it down in a card?"

"No. I want it on the caaaake," she whined.

They both looked at the confection that Melinda had spent hours on, creating a miniature golf course complete with trees, water and even a sand trap. She'd sculpted a marzipan bag of clubs, too, and lined the edges of the cake with little yellow golf tees. On the surface of the water, Mel had written, as instructed, "Happy Birthday, Darling Stanley, from BB with tons of love and kisses."

There was simply no way that she was going to redo the cake for the crazy woman. Mrs. T wanted changes with every order. She was a valuable repeat customer, but she was also a colossal pain in the patooty.

Mel caught Scottie's eye and mouthed a plea for help. He finished arranging a tray of cookies in the bakery case and came over, wiping his hands on his apron. "How long is the poem, Mrs. Temperley?" he asked.

"It's only about six lines."

"Hmm."

Mel had an inspiration. "What if you typed it on a small card, and we stuck it to the front of the cake and then iced a pretty frame for it? Would that work?"

"Well," said Mrs. T, toying with her overly plump bottom lip, "I guess so." She waited a beat. "But can you type it? I don't have time to run home and do that before my nail appointment."

"Sure," Melinda said. "No problem."

"Great. I'll pick it up in an hour, then."

And so Mel found herself using a script font on her computer, typing up BB's Ode to Stanley, her husband.

Just one night on the back nine,
And you were so fine

But I had no clue
That I'd marry you!!!
But all these years later
You're still my Gator
We still burn up a golf cart,
Happy Birthday, dear heart!

Well. Mrs. T wasn't going to win any prizes for her poetry,
that was for sure. It sounded as if she had once had her own
sexcapade. And now Mel couldn't rid her mind of the unwelcome image of BB and Stanley butt naked in a golf cart,
either.

Her mind flashed to a naked Pete instead. *What if I want
to flirt with you, honey? What if I ask you what you're doing
on Saturday?*

She printed out the "poem," such as it was, and carefully
cut it into a small rectangle that she could affix to the cake.
So BB's "One-Night Stan" had ended up becoming her husband…

Mel allowed herself a brief fantasy of herself and Pete
walking down the aisle. In her vision, she wore a size four
Narciso Rodriguez gown, which was about as likely to happen as Pete proposing to her the next time she saw him.

She cringed as she remembered her silly, preteen fantasies about marrying Pete. On the awful day that she'd burped
right in his face, she'd had everything worked out: a ballroom strewn with pink rose petals; the ceiling full of pink
balloons with silver ribbons dangling from them. The tables
were covered with pink cloths and studded with silver candelabra. Even the candles in those were pink. The twelve-year-
old Mel had decided that white was boring.

Her gown, the most important part of the scenario besides
the groom, was exactly like Princess Di's, but pink.

The twenty-five-year-old Mel shuddered. That overblown,

overfestooned dress had been bad enough in cream silk. She knew that now. But back then…

She'd been daydreaming, calculating whom she'd invite to her Big Day—definitely not mean Tiffany Smythe or her snotty sidekick, Heather Delaney—when Pete and Mark had trudged into the house, back from football practice, sweaty and intent on reaching the jar of oatmeal cookies in the kitchen.

Mark ignored her. Pete said, "Hey, Mel. How're you doing?" and winked at her.

The wink was fatal. Her stomach seized up, and her lungs felt filled with tar. She opened her mouth but no sound came out. She could see herself reflected in the shiny oven door, looking like a brain-damaged guppy.

Pete crammed an oatmeal cookie into his own mouth and raised his eyebrows, expecting an answer.

Fine. Say "fine," you moron! But she couldn't.

She was thankful that Mark had buried his head in the refrigerator, probably in search of cold milk.

Pete munched and waited, the corners of his eyes crinkling in friendly amusement.

Mel pressed her front teeth onto her bottom lip and got the "f" out for "fine." She was engaged in a mighty struggle with the "i" when the nervous burp rumbled up her throat and burst like a gunshot into the air.

It was the most awful sound in the history of the planet— until Pete's loud laugh. "S-sorry," he managed, as Melinda's face flash-fried.

The rose petals in her ballroom withered. Her gown wilted and rotted like a cabbage rose in the sun. The balloons popped, and the pink tablecloths went up in flames, charred beyond recognition.

Please, God. Take me now. Pull me through the floor and put me out of my misery. Please…

But the Almighty didn't seem to hear her.

Mark chose that moment to pull his head out of the fridge. "Good one, Bug-Eyes. Was that a burp or a fart?"

Only her brother could have made the moment more calamitous.

Aghast, Melinda turned and fled, her pink and silver dreams destroyed forever.

Total humiliation had obliterated her crush on Pete. She'd never allowed herself to think of him that way again.

Until now.

You idiot. Mel got out her set of piping tips and mixed up some more butter-cream icing to make a frame for BB Temperley's ridiculous Ode.

Pete could easily find her work number, today was Thursday, and he'd shown no signs whatsoever of calling about this Saturday, or any of the other three hundred sixty-four options in the calendar year.

Mel couldn't say she was surprised, no matter what charming things he'd said to her at the wedding breakfast. She let out an involuntary sigh.

As always, her mother had been right.

11

By Friday, Pete's fingers itched to dial Mel's bakery and tell her what a vicious wolverine she had for a mother. He got as far as keying in the number and chewing on the end of the phone's antenna, but he couldn't make himself hit the Send button. He found himself hitting the Off button instead.

Because Melinda would be mortified at her mother's actions. And if she had low self-esteem already, how would she feel to know that her mother had bribed a man to ask her daughter out? It was simple.

Mel would be devastated.

And Pete couldn't do that to her.

Worse, he couldn't even call his best friend, Mark, and vent about the situation, since Jocelyn was also Mark's mother. And because Mark had already threatened to rip off his head and crap down his throat if he so much as laid a hand on Melinda's arm, much less her more luscious and private parts.

Which got Pete to thinking about those again, which filled him with lust as well as frustration and anger.

In desperation, he called his buddy Dev instead, and asked his advice over *choros* and *escabeche de pescado* at a favorite Peruvian restaurant.

Dev looked hungover, which was no big surprise since

he owned a restaurant/bar. Even his dark, spiky hair looked today like it had no energy and was only standing up on his head by sheer virtue of the amount of product smeared into it. He ran a hand down his unshaven face and blinked a couple of times. "Let me get this straight."

Pete waited.

"You banged Mark's sister at the wedding reception?"

"I did not bang her. We—"

Dev waved his fork in the air. "Right, you made mad, passionate, multicolored, many-splendored luuuuv. Whatever. You bumped uglies, and you like her enough to want to call her. But Mama Grizzly is demanding that you call her, and even sweetening the pot if you do."

"Right."

Dev put down his fork and picked up his ice-cold Dos Equis beer instead. He held the bottom of it to each eye for a couple of seconds, then took a swig and set it down. He gazed at Pete across the table as the melted condensation ran from his eyelids. He spread his hands, palms up. "Dude, I don't see the problem."

"What do you mean, you don't see the problem!" Pete stared at him.

"I mean that it's a win-win situation," Dev said, with Satan's own reasonableness.

"It's not!"

"It is. You say you were going to call her anyway. Right?"

"Yeah."

"And this way you even get paid to call her. So freakin' call her, dude!"

"You're advising me to do something completely unethical. You realize that, don't you?"

"Not at all. I'm advising you to do what your heart tells you to do anyway," Dev said. "The other part is just gravy.

Extra. Manna from heaven that's dropped into your lap, like a drunk, horny girl at the tail end of the party."

"Dev, you're so immoral…"

"Not true, my man," he protested. "I'm amoral. There's a difference."

"Yeah? And what's that, buddy?" Pete was disgusted with him.

"It's a big difference. 'Immoral' means that you act against your scruples. 'Amoral' means without scruples. I can't be held accountable for behaving counter to principles that I don't have." Dev flashed him a hundred-megawatt grin.

"I should have known better than to try to talk to you about this," Pete said.

"Pete, Pete, Pete." Dev sighed. "Look, I'm only trying to make you feel better."

"Well, you're making me feel worse, instead."

"Look at it this way, my friend."

"Which way?"

"Can you un-bang Mel, at this point?"

Pete rolled his eyes.

"No, you cannot. Second question. Can you change the fact that Mommie Dearest came to you with her warped deal? No, you cannot. Third question. Will it make Mel feel better if you don't call? Or worse?" Dev gazed at him from those hooded dark eyes of his, unapologetic for making a rude kind of sense.

"Worse," Pete said in gloomy tones.

"Exactly. Now, I ask you, is more business a bad thing? Is more money a bad thing?"

Pete peeled the label off his own beer and stuffed it into one of the empty mussel shells on his plate. He didn't reply.

"The woman's going to take the business somewhere, dude. You may as well get it for Playa Bella. You may as well use her just like she thinks she's using you."

Ugh.

"It's simple payback," Dev explained.

"And what about when it's time to 'let Mel down easy'?" Pete demanded.

"You call the shots."

"What if Jocelyn tries to call them?"

"Tell her in the nicest possible way to get stuffed. After all, she's hardly going to tell her own daughter what she did. The poor girl would never speak to her again. Right?"

Dev had a point.

Still. "I should just walk away now."

"Mmm." Dev lounged back in his chair. "And let Melinda feel used and thrown away by her brother's best friend. Great."

"Shit," Pete said. "Shit, shit, shit."

"Or something like it, anyway." Dev drained his Dos Equis and set it down with a thud. "So what's it gonna be, Dudley?"

Pete squinted at him. "Dudley?"

"Do-Right." Dev belched. "You want that last *choro,* bud?"

"Eat it," Pete said, and watched Dev stick the entire mussel shell in his mouth, then scrape it clean with his front teeth as he pulled it back out. "Then you can eat me, dickhead."

Dev swallowed the food, laughing. "Hey, whatever happened to Mr. Customer Service?"

"He's out to lunch," Pete said, and flipped him the bird. Not that it helped him make a decision.

ON SATURDAY EVENING, Pete drove to Playa Bella, parked, and then met Mr. Reynaldo under the hotel's elegant portico, though he'd much rather be meeting Mel.

Pete had gotten a trim at the barber, shaved carefully, and put on his best dark slacks and crisp white shirt. He'd even shined his shoes. He'd opted out of a tie at the last moment, because Miami was casual and he didn't want to appear to be trying too hard. Evidently, that was a bad decision.

Reynaldo wore a royal blue tie himself, studded with tiny yachts. He looked Pete over from the top of his head to the tips of his shoes and nodded once. Then he said, "Come with me." He turned, went back through the double doors and strolled straight over to Playa Bella's boutique, which sold overpriced golf shirts, baseball hats, ladies' swimwear, jewelry, sundries...and ties.

The manager had locked the glass door and was counting the contents of the cash register. Reynaldo rapped on it with his knuckles. She dropped the money instantly and scurried over to the door. "Yes, Mr. Reynaldo? What can I do for you?"

Pete felt a slow heat burning up his neck as his boss sauntered over to the small tie rack, scanned it and chose a pink-striped one that reminded Pete of a gay zebra in a chorus line.

"Perfecto," Reynaldo said, and handed it to him.

Pete stared at the tie. *I don't get paid enough to wear that. But I might, if I can bring in twenty percent more business.*

He swallowed his bile and his pride, and started to pull off the price tag, which displayed an alarming number of digits after the dollar sign. No wonder the boutique was losing money—its prices were ridiculous.

"No, no," said his boss. "You'll return it tomorrow, eh?"

"Sure," Pete said. Truth to tell, he was glad not to be stuck with the damned thing. He slipped it around his neck and tied it in a simple Windsor knot, tucking the offending tag inside the lining. Who would pay two hundred and seventy-nine dollars for such a butt-ugly rag, anyway?

As they left the gift shop, he told himself to be grateful that Reynaldo hadn't forced him to wear a matching pink silk pocket hankie.

"That place—it's not working," his boss said when they were out of earshot. "The lease is up soon. Find something else to do with the retail space."

"Uh," Pete said. "Sure. No problem." What the hell was he going to do with it? Open a massage parlor?

He made small talk about the Marlins as they drove up to Palm Beach, where the governor's fundraiser was being held.

Reynaldo eased the Bentley past the wrought-iron gates of a long private driveway, at the end of which was a massive, Mediterranean pile with a red barrel-tiled roof. The house was flanked by royal palms and overlooked the ocean.

His boss winked at him. "Not bad, eh? Trump, he used to live a few doors back that way." He jerked a thumb to the left.

"Not bad at all," Pete agreed.

A uniformed maid opened the door, and a white-mustached butler with regal posture led them down a hall the size of a railway station and through a set of double mahogany doors to a ballroom.

The ballroom was full of tables. The tables sparkled with silver flatware and white cloths; the people around them sparkled with gemstones and white teeth. There were senators and mayors and heads of businesses present; there were lawyers and the top brass of various law-enforcement agencies; there were taut, tanned trophy wives milling about, showing off designer clothes and multicarat diamonds. There were people on the make and people on the take.

Reynaldo eased into the crowd, grinning, backslapping, promising Cuban cigars and hot stock tips. He kissed the cheeks of women and winked conspiratorially at the men as he shook hands and murmured greetings. Pete followed in his wake, feeling a little like a barnacle stuck to a whale.

Somehow they ended up at one of the open bars, where Reynaldo ordered him Johnny Walker Black Label, a double, straight up. "You will need it," he said cryptically.

"Rocks," croaked Pete to the bartender. He hated whiskey. If he was going to have to choke the stuff down, he wanted it diluted.

What did Reynaldo mean? He wasn't sure he wanted to know.

Drinks in hand, his boss maneuvered them quite elegantly right into the governor's path. He introduced Pete immediately as his "right-hand man" and Governor Vargas reciprocated, presenting his campaign manager, Gareth Alston. Reynaldo had evidently just met Gareth a couple of days ago.

And within two seconds of shaking Gareth's smooth, limp fingers, Pete was draining his Black Label with full comprehension and horror.

For starters, Gareth had glossier, more buttery-blond highlights than Jocelyn Edgeworth. His personal fragrance was more floral. His cuticles were trimmed more neatly. His nails were buffed to a higher shine.

Then there was the fact that Gareth was retaining Pete's hand with an unexpected strength while he ran his gaze over the breadth of his shoulders, the expanse of his chest and, to Pete's instant outrage, the bulge at his crotch.

"Love the tie," Gareth said, staring far too long at what swung beneath it.

Pete upended the despised glass of whiskey and drained half of it in a gulp. "Thanks." He forced himself to smile. "Yours is nice, too." He flushed uncomfortably. "Your tie."

That was a lie. Alston's tie was a nightmare in violet.

"Dolce & Gabbana," the man purred. "Cost a fortune, but I had to have it."

Pete had never in his life bought a tie on his own. His mother supplied them with depressing regularity on birthdays and at Christmas. He'd never had the heart to tell her that most of the ties were still in their boxes in his closet.

As for Alston's tie, he wouldn't use it to clean his windshield. But Pete smiled and nodded as Gareth went on and on about the high-end shops at Bal Harbor. "I'm a Neiman's addict," the guy enthused, as Pete took another sip of his despised Johnny Walker Black Label.

He choked on it as he lowered his glass and saw Melinda. Worse, some of the whiskey dribbled out of his mouth and onto the pink tie as he coughed and hacked.

And the noise drew not only her attention, but that of his boss, who frowned at him from across the room.

Within moments, Melinda made her way over from the elaborate dessert table she'd evidently been supervising. "You look as if you could use this," she said, as she proffered a starched linen napkin.

"Thanks," Pete wheezed, and held it to his mouth.

She seemed fixated on his tie.

He, in turn, was fixated on the plunging neckline of her black cocktail dress. How well he remembered the contents…

Pete wrapped up his coughing attack. "Uh, Melinda Edgeworth, meet Gareth Alston, Governor Vargas's campaign manager. Gareth, Melinda is a very fine pastry chef."

"Thank you. Mrs. Van der Voort was nice enough to ask me to do the desserts for the party tonight."

"Oh?" Alston displayed a set of perfect, bleached teeth. "Sunny is a doll, isn't she?"

Melinda nodded.

As Pete looked down to blot the whiskey from his tie, he realized that the price tag had popped out during his coughing fit. Heat and mortification surged up his neck.

Gareth Alston gave a small snort.

"Oh, Pete," Melinda exclaimed after a beat. "I'm so sorry! The price tag was still on Mark's tie."

He blinked.

Mel reached up and yanked off the tag, crumpling it in her hand. Then she turned to Alston. "Poor Pete called me en route, because he didn't know until too late that he needed a tie for the party. I snagged one of my brother's for him—they've been best friends since junior high."

"Well, wasn't that nice of you," Gareth said.

Yes, it certainly was. Pete could have kissed her then and there, for more than one reason.

"I haven't had a chance to call you," he said. "Sorry."

The concern and amusement in her eyes faded to something flat, polite and cold. "No worries."

"It was fabulous chatting with you, Pete," Alston said. "If you'll excuse me…" And he moved into the crowd.

"Thank you," Pete said to her. "You have no idea how grateful I am to you. No idea."

She shrugged. "It was nothing."

"Really. So…Mel, you look beautiful."

Her face froze. "Pete, please don't."

"Don't what?"

"Don't pay me compliments, okay?" Her lips, moments ago a lush bowed shape, flattened into a thin line. "And you also don't need to pretend you were going to call. It's okay. I'm a big girl."

He caught the bitterness in that last sentence; the double meaning. "Mel, you don't understand—"

She put a hand on his arm. "Pete. I do understand. We had a good time. It's cool. Now, forget it."

12

PETE SHOVED THE PRICE TAG deep into the pocket of his trousers, downed the last of the whiskey and set the empty glass on a passing waiter's tray. He hated being this twisted up inside. He was a human pretzel.

Melinda had come unexpectedly and gracefully to his rescue, but then turned into an ice queen and retreated. If it didn't make absolutely no sense, he'd have sworn that the word *beautiful* had triggered her cold response. But in his experience, women adored being told they were beautiful. Did he need to enroll in Female Behavior and Habits 101?

If only such a class existed.

He watched Melinda's shapely backside as she fled to her dessert table and gave instructions to the redheaded guy who was clearly there to help her. They had left a large rectangular spot on the table blank, while to either side were mouthwatering tarts, stemmed crystal goblets filled with chocolate mousse, cookies in all shapes and sizes. A silver urn at one end held coffee.

Mel nodded at something the redheaded guy said and flashed a smile at him. A smile that Pete wanted to be his, not some leprechaun twerp's. Threatening brother or not. Wolverine mother or not.

He plucked two glasses of red wine off yet another waiter's tray and made his way purposefully over to her. Her back still to him, he leaned over her shoulder and angled his head so that his mouth was only inches from her ear. "I don't want to forget it."

She jumped, clearly startled.

"Do you?" Pete asked, as she whirled to face him.

"Yes." Then she spoiled the finality of her message by snatching one of the glasses of wine, taking a furtive look around, and downing a third of it. Evidently she didn't want to be seen drinking on the job.

"I saw that!" said the leprechaun assistant, popping out of nowhere.

At the same time, Pete leaned in toward her again and said, "I don't believe you."

Mel hunched her shoulders defensively against both of them, while for the second time that night, Pete became the target of a not-so-subtle evaluation by another male. Actually a third time, if he counted the ordeal with Reynaldo and the tie.

"Aren't you going to introduce me to your very handsome friend?" the leprechaun asked from behind a naughty smile.

"Scottie, this is Pete. Pete, Scottie."

Scottie put his hands on his hips and tsked. "Now, Mel, that's like handing someone a naked, un-iced cookie. Details, please!"

She closed her eyes for a second, then opened them and sighed. "Scottie is my very talented, very nosy assistant at the bakery. He's masterful with fondant—"

"Oooh, masterful!" Scottie preened. "I like that word."

"—and he's trying to steal my dog through culinary bribery."

"Who's Fon-Don?" Pete asked.

Scottie snickered.

"Fondant," Mel said, emphasizing the "t." "It's a type of icing."

"Got it."

"Pete, here," Mel continued to Scottie, "is an old friend of my brother's who used to call me Bug-Eyes and once trapped me for hours in a tree house."

"Not my idea," protested Pete. "It was Mark's."

"Bug-Eyes?" repeated Scottie. "Hey, can I steal that?"

"No." Melinda glared at him.

"Sure." Pete grinned.

"We used to call him Fozzie," Mel informed her assistant. "Feel free to steal that, too."

"Well, I'm damn glad to meet you, Fozzie." The leprechaun stuck out his hand with an impish smile. "Did you get the name because you have a hairy back?"

"Excuse me?"

"You two deserve each other," Mel said, and drained the rest of her wine before walking out of the room.

"The ingratitutde!" Pete said, mock-offended. "She drinks the wine I bring her and leaves." He cupped a hand to his mouth. "Thank you, Pete, that cabernet was delicious," he called after her.

To Scottie, he said, "No, I do not have a hairy back, not that it's any of your business."

Scottie laughed. "So, do you have designs on my boss?"

"She wasn't kidding, was she? You are nosy." But Pete poked his tongue into his cheek, softening his words.

"Yup. So do you?"

"If you mean do I want to ask her out, then yes."

"Well, then, what are you waiting for?"

"Your permission, of course," Pete said in dry tones.

"Granted. But only if you're nice to her."

"Oh, I figure I'll kick her like a can down the street and then into the nearest dive bar, where I'll get her drunk on cheap tequila and then take advantage of her," Pete said with heavy sarcasm. "That okay with you?"

"You'd best not be doing that," Scottie warned. "I may be small, but I can damn sure pick a lock and hide a nest of hornets under your toilet lid."

Pete blinked. "I think we understand each other. Pleasure to meet you." He stuck out his hand.

Scottie's grip was firm and dry. "There are a lot of people who care about Mel."

"Yeah. I'm one of them, buddy, so you can save your hornet surprise for somebody else, 'kay?"

"Okay."

After that interesting conversation, Pete went in search of Mel. The girl sure had a talent for disappearing at parties.

MEL TOLD HERSELF that she wasn't hiding from Pete. She was simply transporting a cake almost bigger than she was. A cake she'd made to resemble the Governor's Mansion in Tallahassee, Florida, surrounded by lush, sculpted-sugar landscaping and even tiny marzipan people. Across the front of the façade ran a banner that proclaimed, "Governor Vargas, Term Two!"

She had the cake on a wheeled service cart that she used for these occasions.

"Mel, is that you behind the mansion?"

She couldn't actually see Pete through the baked architecture, since she was bent forward, pushing the cart, but that was his voice. She stood up straight and peered over the gabled roof. "No, it's King Kong."

"Would you like some help moving that? It's incredible, by the way."

"Thanks, but I'm used to doing this by now. Watch your feet."

"You don't want to sweep me off them?"

"Not so much. I don't want to roll over your toes, either."

"Melinda, you're going to have to talk to me at some point. So you may as well go out with me."

"Wow, Pete." She raised her eyebrows and kept rolling the steel cart towards the ballroom. "I think that might be the most gracious invitation I've ever received. And the most heartfelt." She picked up speed as she went down the cavernous hallway, but he kept pace with her easily.

"Don't you get sarcastic with me, Bug-Eyes."

"Wouldn't dream of it, Fozzie."

"Mel, at the wedding breakfast, I asked what you were doing tonight before I realized that I had to come to this party."

"And as I recall, my mother showed up before I could tell you that I had to come to this party. Anyway, I told you already, you're off the hook."

"But the point I'm trying to make, Melinda, is that I don't want to be off the hook," Pete said. "I want to see you again."

"Could you be sweet and get the door for me?"

"Sure, but that's not an answer."

"What was the question, exactly?" Mel stalled for time.

Pete positioned himself right in front of the doors to the ballroom so that she couldn't get past him. "Will you go on a date with me?"

He looked sincere, his face open and honest, his gray eyes holding absolutely no guile. He also looked muscular, and despite the Pepto-Bismol-pink striped tie, hot. She remembered exactly how he looked, smelled and felt naked.

"If you will get out of the way, open the door for me, and promise never to wear that ridiculous and criminally expensive tie again, then yes—I'll go on a date with you."

Pete nodded once, threw open the doors and got out of the way. "I can explain the tie," he said as Mel passed him with the edible Governor's Mansion.

"I sure hope so." She gave it a tug as she passed.

He leaned into her space and whispered, "And by the way, since you yanked off the price tag I can't return it now. So I'm gonna use it to blindfold you or tie you to my bed."

Mel felt the blush start at her chest and rise all the way up her neck before flourishing in her cheeks. "Promises, promises," was all she said.

And then people began to notice the cake coming in. They turned to applaud.

There was nothing like a ballroom full of guests clapping for a woman to make her feel good, but Mel knew that most of her elation stemmed from one simple fact: that Pete wanted to see her again.

Mel smiled and nodded her thanks for the appreciation. Then she and Scottie eased the huge cake off the cart and into the space on the table that they'd designated for it. Now their job was to disappear quickly and cede the spotlight to Governor Vargas, who was stepping up to the podium and microphone in the corner.

Mel's preference had been to set up the cake before everyone got there, but Mrs. Van der Voort was a friend of her mother's, and had wanted to give her a little attention so she'd get more business.

She found Sunny Van der Voort in the crowd, kissed her cheek and whispered her thanks as the governor began his speech.

"I've already had close to a dozen people ask me for your business card, honey. Do you have any more?"

Mel nodded. "In my purse. I'll go get some." She threaded her way through the room as the lights dimmed and Vargas told everyone how honored he was by their presence.

The audience ate it up, even though they'd paid five hundred dollars a plate to be here. Melinda was surprised but relieved that her parents weren't in attendance. She didn't think she could handle any more of her mother for a while.

She was walking past an alcove that held an old-fashioned telephone desk when she glimpsed a flash of pink snaking through the air. Mel yelped in surprise. Next thing she knew she'd been lassoed and yanked into the small space.

"Gotcha!" said Pete, pulling her against his chest.

She struggled briefly. "You scared me!"

"Sorry."

"And aren't we a little too old to be playing Cowboys and Indians?"

"Not at all," he said, spinning her around and planting a smooch on her. He used the fact that her mouth was open to slide his tongue inside and kiss her until she was breathless.

"Pete! What is the meaning of this?"

"Dunno," he said. "Does it have to have a meaning, other than me wanting to kiss you?"

She changed the subject. "I agreed to go out on a date with you, not to be manhandled at a political fundraiser."

"Huh. So it's going to be a completely kissless date?"

"I didn't say that…"

"Good. Kissless dates suck, if you want my opinion."

"Pete, why were you wearing that ugly tie with the price tag still on it, and why is it now around my shoulders?"

"My boss borrowed it from the Playa Bella Boutique because he wanted me to wear it. And I'm supposed to be flirting, I think, with Vargas's campaign manager. Which rubs me the wrong way, since I'm not gay."

"O-kaaay."

"So I'd rather rub you the right way." He grinned at her.

"Nobody's rubbing anyone at the moment." Mel eyed him severely. "So it was your boss who picked out the tie? He has really terrible taste."

Pete's grin disappeared. "No, that's the thing—he doesn't. He has excellent taste. He picked that particular tie to send a message. I'm supposed to become Gareth Alston's bitch, so that we'll get a bunch of the governor's fundraisers booked at Playa Bella."

Mel stared at him. "Are you saying Reynaldo expects you to…"

"Not gonna happen," Pete said definitively. "Absolutely not. But I'm in a bind, that's for sure. I don't know what to do."

"Hmm." Mel eyed him thoughtfully. "Maybe what you need, Fozzie, is a redheaded boyfriend to protect your honor."

"No, no, no—"

Pete was still protesting when she slipped the tie "lasso" off her shoulders, threw it over his head and tightened the noose. Disregarding everything he had to say, she towed him outside and called Scottie on her cell phone.

13

"Scottie," Mel said into the phone.

"No," Pete said again, forcefully.

"I need you to—"

Pete grabbed the cell phone from her hand and hit the End Call button.

"Wow. That was really rude, Mr. Customer Service."

"Yeah, it was. Sorry, Mel. But I don't want a redheaded boyfriend."

She raised an eyebrow. "Redheaded girlfriend?"

"Nope. I'd prefer a brunette, thanks."

Mel rolled her eyes. "May I have my phone back, please?"

Pete grinned. "I don't know. What will you give me in return?"

"In return, I won't call security and tell them that you've stolen my property." She held out her hand.

"That's cold." Pete took her hand, pulled her close to him and looked down into her face. A second ago he'd been teasing her, his eyes crinkled at the corners. Now they'd gone serious on her.

"Hey, Beautiful," he said, and paused as if he were gauging her reaction. "Thanks for trying to help me out, though. Again."

If offer card is missing write to: The Reader Service, P.O. Box 1867, Buffalo NY 14240-1867 or visit www.ReaderService.com

NO POSTAGE
NECESSARY
IF MAILED
IN THE
UNITED STATES

BUSINESS REPLY MAIL
FIRST-CLASS MAIL   PERMIT NO. 717   BUFFALO, NY

POSTAGE WILL BE PAID BY ADDRESSEE

THE READER SERVICE

PO BOX 1867

BUFFALO NY 14240-9952

Get FREE BOOKS and a FREE GIFT when you play the...

LAS VEGAS GAME

Just scratch off the gold box with a coin. Then check below to see the gifts you get!

YES! I have scratched off the gold box. Please send me my **2 FREE BOOKS** and **gift for which I qualify.** I understand that I am under no obligation to purchase any books as explained on the back of this card.

151/351 HDL FNTR

FIRST NAME

LAST NAME

ADDRESS

APT.#

CITY

STATE/PROV.

ZIP/POSTAL CODE

7 7 7 Worth TWO FREE BOOKS plus a BONUS Mystery Gift!

Worth TWO FREE BOOKS!

TRY AGAIN!

Offer limited to one per household and not applicable to series that subscriber is currently receiving. All orders subject to credit approval. Please allow 4 to 6 weeks for delivery.

She stiffened. That word.

I'll bet he told you that you were beautiful, didn't he? And you took your dress right off for him.

"Yeah, no problem." She tried to tug her hand away.

"Why don't you like that word, Melinda?"

"What word?" She played dumb as she continued to struggle against the strength of his grip.

"Beautiful," he repeated.

She fumbled for an answer, anything but the truth. "Because it's generic," she said. "It's overused. It's—"

Pete shook his head. "That's not why," he said flatly. "Something about that word causes you pain."

"Don't be ridiculous."

"I'm not. I know what I'm talking about."

Her hackles rose with her defenses. "Oh, so you're a mind reader?"

"Nope. But I can read your face. And when I say that particular word, your features turn to stone. You won't meet my gaze. Your lips flatten into a narrow line, as if you're trying to make them disappear."

"Yeah, whatever."

"And you know what else?" Pete continued.

"No, please tell me. You clearly know lots more about me than I do myself."

He smoothly overrode her sarcasm. "When I say that particular word, your shoulders hunch forward as if you're trying to camouflage your breasts. You fold your arms across your body. You even turn your toes a little inward. You hang your head so that your hair hides your face."

She sighed. "Fine."

"Huh uh. It's not fine." And he bent his head to kiss her.

Mel let it happen. His lips brushed hers lightly at first, almost tenderly. He let go of her hand and trailed his fingers along her nape, up into her hairline. Then he began to kiss her as if he meant it.

He smelled faintly of whiskey, of his breezy aftershave, of the starch in his laundered shirt. Best of all, he smelled like himself, the scent intensely familiar, somehow.

A longing built within her, deep inside. Pete turned his head to kiss her neck, and the beard shadow on his face scraped the tender skin at her throat.

Breathless, Mel was torn between urging him on and needing to push him away. "We can't do this here," she managed to say.

"Mmm." He stopped any further words with his mouth, his tongue exploring hers. He sucked on her bottom lip; slipped a hand under a breast to cup it.

"Stop, Pete—"

But he ignored her and slid his hand up her skirt.

To her shame, she didn't immediately knock it away. Mr. Customer Service knew exactly what he was doing.

"Okay, stop, Pete. Not here. Not now."

He gave a muffled protest against her cleavage, but removed his hand from the happy zone and stood up straight, locking his fingers behind his neck. "Why do you always do this to me in public?"

"Huh?" Mel clued in then, dropping her gaze to the tent under his belt buckle. "How is that in any way my fault? You kissed me."

"You incited me," Pete said, his mouth quirking up at the corners.

Mel got indignant. "I did no such thing!"

"Yes, you did. Because you're so off-putting in that low-cut, low-down black dress of yours…"

"Off-putting?!"

"Extremely so. In fact, I do think you may be the ugliest woman I've ever encountered."

Mel gasped. "What did you say?"

"Troll-like, in fact. But I've always had a thing for trolls. Gnomes, too, if you want the truth." Pete nodded, his face completely deadpan.

Mel began to laugh in the face of this outrageousness. "You—you—you cannot—"

Pete spread his hands, palms up. "Is there a problem?"

"You just told me I was ugly! That's not okay."

"But you hate it when I call you beautiful. And now I'm not allowed to call you off-putting or ugly. Jeez! What's Mr. Customer Service, here, to do?"

"Okay, Pete, you've made your point."

He lifted an eyebrow. "All I want to do is please you, honey."

"Then let me go inside and do my job."

He sighed. "I suppose that means I need to go in, too, and see to mine. But what are you doing later?"

She shot him a look from under her lashes. "Another booty call, Pete?"

"It's not meant that way, and you know it, Melinda." He fished her cell phone out of his pocket and tossed it to her. "My number's now programmed into that, just so you know."

"Gee, I wonder how that happened?" But Mel shot him a smile over her shoulder as she walked up the steps of the big house.

"Couldn't tell you," Pete said.

She left him waiting outside until the tent in his pants subsided.

PETE HAD TAKEN four steps back into the ballroom of Mrs. Van der Voort's vast house when Reynaldo spotted him and beckoned him over to where he stood with Alston and a couple of fat-cat attorneys. Dutifully, Pete went.

"There you are, Pedro," said Reynaldo genially. "Gareth,

here, was just telling me how extremely impressed Governor Vargas was with his State Capitol cake this evening."

"Wasn't that incredible?" Pete exclaimed. "A friend of mine, Melinda Edgeworth, did it. She's so talented."

"I was just explaining to Gareth that we're in the process of negotiating with Melinda to bring her on board as our pastry chef at Playa Bella," Reynaldo added.

Pete choked. "Uh, right," he said, trying to recover. "Yes, indeed. The negotiations are a little complicated because she does have her own shop, though." He shot a significant glance at his boss. "And needless to say, she's building quite a name for herself."

Reynaldo waved a hand. "Yes, but this is Playa Bella, Miami's premier luxury hotel. Not to mention the other jewels in the Reynaldo crown. She will jump at the chance."

"I certainly hope so, sir."

"Pedro. One does not negotiate with hope," Reynaldo said expansively. "It's a war, my boy. One negotiates with…how you say?…brass balls—and brass knuckles."

A war…knuckles. Pete had a brief flashback to his childhood; his brother and his teeth on the floor in a pool of blood; his father roaring with pain and clutching his own fist.

The fat-cat attorneys and Gareth Alston chuckled, bringing Pete back to the present.

"A war. Absolutely," Pete agreed, then chuckled right along with them. He tried to tamp down his rising dislike of his boss. In his own way, the man was as big a bully as Pete's father had been. And he, Pete, hated himself just as much for placating him; constantly avoiding conflict.

"Besides," his boss added, "she is only a girl. *Dios mio,* offer her free use of the spa, free silk-wraps on her nails, and she will fall at your feet."

Pete choked for the second time, especially since he'd just spotted Melinda out of the corner of his eye. She was well within hearing range, chatting with an older couple. She smiled at them, kissed each of them on the cheek, and moved away. She then turned to shoot Pete a look that would eviscerate the entire Navy Seal Team Six.

She'd clearly heard the entire exchange from where she'd stood, approximately three feet away. Beautiful. Just beautiful. And yes, Pete did get the irony of that word popping into his head—because this was going to be a very ugly situation.

He looked down at his feet. "Actually, sir, I don't think Melinda wears those silk wrap things on her nails. You know, because she's got her hands in batters and icings all day."

Reynaldo cast his eyes heavenward. "So offer her free massages, then. These are silly details. You will get them worked out."

"Of course. No problem." Pete produced a sickly smile to match his sickly tie. "Now, if you'll excuse me for a moment?" He felt like a ten-year-old asking to get up from the dinner table.

His boss waved him off, and he made his escape.

MELINDA FELT SURE that her head could function as a rice-cooker at the moment, because steam was coming out of her ears. How dare that man? And Pete had just stood there, grinning like a jack-o'-lantern.

Her more rational side reminded her that the guy was probably his boss. But still...

"I take one step forward with you, and then two steps back," Pete's voice said behind her.

She turned. "Got your brass knuckles on?"

He winced. "Heh."

"Or do you think your brass balls will be enough to persuade me?"

Pete rubbed the back of his neck. "Uh—"

"That man," Melinda stated not so quietly, "is a brass knucklehead. Who does he think he is?"

"A major hotelier."

"I don't even know what to say to you. What was that all about? It started with a lie—that we're already negotiating—and ended with an insult. I'm just a girl."

"He's from another culture and another generation," Pete said, employing tact. "He's very…traditional."

Mel snorted. "That's a great euphemism for chauvinist asshole."

"Please keep your voice down?"

"Why?"

Pete sent her a speaking look. "Instead of being insulted, Mel, try looking at the situation as a true compliment. Evidently you have very much impressed the governor with the cake. And my boss takes that seriously. He'd like to offer you a job."

"As you mentioned to him, I do have my own business. Why would I give up my freedom to work for someone else?"

"We'd make it very much worth your while."

"No offense, Pete, but I did a couple of gigs for big hotels right out of culinary school. Those jobs weren't exactly little slices of heaven."

"Playa Bella's not just any big hotel. It's—"

"I know, I know, it has a spa! Where I could get my nails done." She shook her head.

Pete sighed inwardly.

"Can you imagine what would happen to my business," Mel said conversationally, "if a silk-wrapped nail tip turned up in someone's cake?"

"Yeah, that would be bad. But free massages could be nice," Pete pointed out, trying to lighten the atmosphere.

"That man can massage my big butt," Mel fumed.

"It's not big," Pete said. "It's just right. I happen to like it very much."

"And you. You are a…a…" She fumbled for the right words.

Pete raised his eyebrows and waited expectantly.

"…a professional soother."

His lips twitched. "You make it sound so dirty, Mel."

She frowned at him. "It is."

He grinned back. "Well, if I'm dirty and you're ugly, what say we meet up after the party and work toward getting down-right nasty?"

Reluctantly she laughed. "You need to stop calling me 'ugly.' It's not good for a girl's ego."

"Honey, as I said, you've left me no alternative. You hate being called beau—"

Mel held up a hand. "Don't say it."

"As I recall from last weekend, 'gorgeous' made you even more uncomfortable."

Melinda sighed. "You're not going to drop this, are you?" She could feel herself blushing.

"How about 'pretty'? Would that be so terrible? Can I call you 'pretty,' Mel?" His gray eyes were steady, serious behind the twinkle they held.

She shifted her weight uncomfortably from one foot to the other.

"Can I?"

"Yes, Pete. You can call me that." She fidgeted with her bracelet. "Thank you."

"Okay, Pretty Melinda." He reached out and took her hand in his big, warm one. "Now, pretty-please, can we meet up for a drink after the party?"

When he looked at her like that, when he stroked her palm with his thumb in that way and sent a shiver up her spine, he was irresistible. So much so that he could probably talk her into serving a jail sentence for him, despite the fact that she knew she'd just been professionally soothed and expertly charmed.

"Yes, Pete." Funny how his face lit up at those two words. "I'll have a drink with you later—as long as you don't give me a sales pitch on Playa Bella."

"Who, me?" Pete did his best to look innocent, but failed miserably.

She had a feeling she was in for a long night. But not once did she admit that, in the face of Gutierrez's lost business, the Playa Bella offer wasn't entirely unappealing.

14

PETE SOON DISCOVERED that "meeting up" with Melinda to have that drink was complicated. First, he had to extricate himself from the return trip with Reynaldo in his Bentley.

"What is that country saying, Pedro?" his boss mused. "Leave with the one you dance with?"

He would make this difficult. Pete ran a finger around the inside of his collar. "Ha, ha!"

"Ha, ha." Reynaldo squinted from behind his fat Cuban cigar.

"Uh, I believe it's, 'Dance with the one you brought,' sir."

"And have we danced, Peter? Or should I ask—have you danced with those you should, this evening?"

He meant Gareth Alston. Pete shuddered at a mental image of him and Alston twined in a tango. *Never gonna happen. I'd as soon French-kiss a flamingo.*

"My dance card's been very productive tonight, Mr. Reynaldo. I'll follow up with Gary, in particular, this week."

"Gary, eh?" His boss chuckled and took a deep pull on the Cuban. "I'm delighted to hear it."

But I won't pretend to be gay, you son of a bitch. He didn't say the words aloud. It didn't seem necessary, given his reasons for not riding back with the man. "So, I'll see you Monday, then."

"You and your zipper, Pedro. Ah, to be young again..."

Pete forced himself to give Reynaldo a purely male, conspiratorial wink, even though it didn't feel right. It disgusted him, frankly. "Good night, sir."

"Good night, Señor Casanova."

Shoving aside his irritation at that dig, Pete hunted down Melinda and found himself heading back to Miami in her white bakery van, with the scent of sugar and vanilla in his nostrils and Scottie wedged behind them.

"Isn't this romantic?" Scottie quipped. "The moon, the stars, the double yellow lines..."

Despite the very normal urge to stuff the little leprechaun into the nearest pot of gold, Pete had to chuckle.

"Just the three of us, in perfect harmony," Scottie sighed.

Melinda cast him a speaking glance, but Scottie blithely ignored it. He was having too much fun.

"There's something so slick and sexy about a minivan, don't you agree? And there's room to rumble, if you know what I mean."

Pete stared out the windshield, refusing to egg him on.

"Much better than, say, a cramped sports car. No contortions necessary, no accidental penetration by the gearshift—"

Pete shuddered and clenched involuntarily.

"Scottie," said Mel, clearly outraged.

"Well, it's happened, I swear!"

"I so do not want to hear about it."

"Not to me, you understand, but to a friend of a friend."

"Riiiiight," Pete said.

"It wasn't me!"

"Uh-huh."

"So." Scottie seemed to feel the need for a subject change. "Who was that handsome devil you were talking to?"

Pete drew a blank. "Which handsome devil?"

"That guy with the governor."

"Gareth Alston? The one in the awful purple tie?"

Scottie nodded. "The gorgeous, violet Dolce & Gabbana tie."

Mel dug Pete in the ribs.

"Right," Pete said hastily. "That's what I meant."

"So? Who is he? I like his style."

"Alston is Governor Vargas's campaign manager." Pete paused, guiltily wondering how he could spin this to his advantage. "Would you like to meet him?"

"Oh, no. I have a boyfriend," Scottie said, in tones that could only be described as gloomy.

Still, Pete's hopes were dashed.

"Scottie, how many deliveries do we have tomorrow?" Mel asked, in the ensuing silence.

"Four, I think. Oh, and did I tell you that Mrs. Temperley called to say that Stanley loved his golf course cake?"

"Great," Mel said. "So, can you do the deliveries tomorrow? Or do I need to call Roberto?"

"No, I can do them."

"Thanks."

"*De nada,* Mistress Mel."

They dropped off Scottie at his Brickell high-rise and headed to The Blue Martini, a popular upscale bar in the area, where they sat at the curved bar bathed in blue light and ordered two of the signature martinis, which arrived with glow sticks in them.

Mel's dark hair glinted in the deep azure glow of the place, and her eyes seemed larger and more mysterious. She looked to Pete like a voluptuous 1950s film star, and he couldn't get enough of her full lips as they molded against the rim of her glass.

He remembered them molded against him as she'd taken

him into her mouth, and an electric current shot through him, eddying out at his groin. She truly seemed to have no idea how sexy she was, as she toyed with the glow stick in her drink.

"So tell me, Mel," he said. "How did you get into the cake business?"

She lifted a shoulder. "I always loved to bake as a kid—cookies, cupcakes, pies."

"Did you learn from your mom?"

"My mom? No. She's never really baked."

Pete frowned. "But I remember those amazing oatmeal-raisin cookies she used to make."

Mel poked her tongue into her cheek. "She didn't make those. Our maid, Miss Alfie, did. You remember her?"

"Yeah, I do…" Pete remembered a large lady who always wore white T-shirts under sleeveless cotton dresses. She had skin the color of milk chocolate, blunt features and kind eyes. "She was always very patient with us kids. Made us wash our hands a lot."

Mel smiled. "I'm still in touch with Miss Alfie, even though she hasn't worked for my parents in years. I adore her."

"So you learned to bake from her?"

Melinda nodded. "I used to ask her all kinds of questions, like why a glop of cookie dough would spread out flat in the oven. Or what made dough rise. Or why cakes were round or square but not triangular. She'd always do her best to answer. Never shooed me away." She smiled.

"She'd let me 'help,' too. Taught me how to crack an egg, even though I made a lot of messes for her to clean up." Mel took a sip of her martini and looked at him.

"I still can't crack one right. I usually end up with bits of shell in my scrambled eggs," he said ruefully. "I'm kitchen-challenged. I can't even make microwave popcorn without burning it."

Mel laughed. "But you can take apart a car engine?"

"Yes, but that's different. I can put one back together, too."

She shook her head. "I remember you and Mark working on that old Impala."

He nodded. "The green machine." He'd slept in the backseat of that car on more nights than he cared to remember, escaping the ugly confrontations between his father and brother—and his brother's need to take out his helpless rage on Pete afterward. Dad never laid a finger on their mother, but Brent had been a big kid with an inability to keep his mouth shut—and had taken a lot of physical punishment for it. Pete had learned at a very early age to either make nice or disappear when that wasn't possible.

"You loved that car."

"Yeah, I did. It was my escape chute back then."

"Escape from what?"

"Oh, you know. Stuff." Pete shifted the subject away from himself. "So back to cakes. How do you—I don't know the right word for it—construct? How do you build one like the governor's cake tonight? Because that wasn't just baking—it was architecture and landscaping. The thing was a work of art. You didn't just pour it into a mold and pop it out on a tray."

"I have some shortcuts and tools," Mel admitted.

"Such as?"

"Well, for example I use a ready-made cake board for the base. And when I stack the different levels, I use ready-made bases, too. And the columns—those are molded plastic. I order them out of a catalogue."

"But the trees, the bushes and flowers, the tiny people?"

"A lot of that I mold out of sugar-paste or marzipan, but you can order some ready-made things, too."

"Nazi-what?"

Mel laughed. "M-a-r-z-i-p-a-n. Marzipan. It's made out of almond paste and sugar."

"Almond paste. Right." Pete wrinkled his nose. "Sounds weird."

"It's not weird. It's delicious."

"I'll take your word for it. So were you an art major?"

"No. Business."

"Then how'd you learn to sculpt things like that?"

"You get a lot of practice in culinary school," she said wryly. "And you also have to sample everything you make, so your education isn't helpful to your figure."

Pete wasn't about to let the conversation go down that path again. "I love your figure. I've been dreaming about it, if you want to know the truth."

Even in the eerie blue lighting, he could see Mel blush. She took a quick sip of her martini.

"You're hot, Melinda Edgeworth. There—is that an acceptable word?"

The blush intensified.

"Like a dark-haired, dark-eyed Marilyn Monroe."

She looked up and met his gaze, her eyes faintly disbelieving but questioning, too.

Pete nodded.

After another martini, her disbelief dissipated somewhat, and a smile tried to break free around the curve of her lips. He was getting through to her. Pete leaned forward, into her space.

"I want to cover you in whipped cream and lick it off," he whispered. "Or chocolate syrup. Maybe both."

She squirmed in her seat and he used her reaction to his advantage. "I'd like to eat your cupcake, sweetheart."

"Pete!"

"In fact, I think we should finish our drinks and stop at a mini-mart for some Insta-Wip on the way back to your place."

Mel recoiled. "Absolutely not," she said, as his face fell in disappointment.

She poked him. "If you're going to cover me in whipped cream, it's not going to be a disgusting fake substitute. It's going to be the real thing. With a little sugar and vanilla added."

He laughed. "I guess you don't believe in store-bought chocolate syrup, either?"

She shook her head. "Won't touch it. Mine is much better."

"Can we make it naked?"

She tilted her head and considered him for a moment. "Maybe."

"Or better yet, you could wear an apron and nothing else?"

"And you can wear my toque."

"Your what?"

"Chef's hat."

"You have one?"

"Of course."

"Then what are we waiting for?" Pete slid off his barstool and stood up.

"It would be a good thing to pay for our drinks," Melinda reminded him, reaching into her purse.

"Oh, right…" Pete frowned at her as he dug for his wallet. "What do you think you're doing? You're not paying."

"Well, I didn't want to just assume that—"

"Assume," Pete said firmly. "You will never pick up a tab if you're out with me. Not once. Got it?"

"Well—"

"You're too pretty to pay." He winked at her. "How's that for chauvinistic? Huh? See, I can be traditional, too."

Mel dimpled.

"Now, let's go find the dairy section in the nearest grocery store. Because, damn, woman! You've done it to me again."

Mel looked down at the all-too-familiar tent in his pants

and pursed her lips playfully. "Do you have this problem with all the girls?"

He shook his head and answered honestly. "No. Only with you, Melinda. Only with you."

15

TWO MARTINIS LATER, they stood in Mel's kitchen. Pete found that vodka was very helpful in forgetting guilt. It did a great job of anesthetizing his conscience and making him forget that not only did he have a secret "deal" with Jocelyn, but an assignment to manipulate Mel on behalf of his boss.

Here he was, in her kitchen, ogling her mostly naked body.

"What would Grandma say?" Mel asked.

She'd put on for Pete one of that dearly departed lady's vintage aprons, a white-lace thong and a pair of high heels that could only be described as slutty. Pete loved them.

"Let's leave Grandma out of this picture," he suggested, his mouth going dry at the view as Melinda bent to retrieve her electric mixer from a cabinet.

Evidently because her father's sister hadn't wanted them, Mel had inherited a box of her grandmother's table linens and aprons, which she treasured and kept starched and ironed for use at dinner parties. Not that she threw many.

But when she did, she informed Pete, she had them the old-fashioned way, handing out tiny embroidered cocktail napkins with the drinks; using silver candelabra and the rest of Grandma's linens.

The apron she wore now was made of blue gingham with

a white cotton panel inset in front, which was dotted with big daisies. It had wide blue gingham straps that slipped over the shoulders, Mel's spectacular breasts bare and showcased between them. The apron strings, also of gingham, tied in a bow at the back, right over her lacy little thong and cheeky cheeks. Pete wanted to take a bite out of one. He was down-right slobbering and not ashamed to admit it.

Then there were the shoes: strappy red-patent leather sandals, sky-high, that made her legs look twice as long and triggered all kinds of dirty fantasies in him.

"Okay, but poor little Mami is truly shocked. She'll never recover from seeing me like this."

Pete shook his head. He'd just made Mami's acquaintance, kneeling to let Her Highness sniff him from toes to crotch. She'd deigned to accept a tiny, pink-frosted doughnut from Mel—one with colored sprinkles, no less. The dog had a lit-tle yellow-canopied bed in the living room, with tiny yellow sheets and pillows.

Since Mami, tucked into a corner, had focused all nine of her pounds on gnawing a designer bone of some kind, Pete doubted any lasting damage to her psyche. "She's seen you come out of the shower before, right?"

"Yes, but that's different."

"Not to a dog, it's not. I promise."

"You're probably right…so why do I feel like the corrup-tor of canine youth and innocence?"

"You're just self-conscious. How old is she?" Pete asked.

"Seven."

"Then in dog years, Mami is forty-nine. She's been around the block a few times. She's not shocked."

Melinda lived in a small townhome in Coconut Grove, a once funky/artsy section of Miami that was becoming gen-trified despite resistance. She'd explained that she'd chosen the place for its gourmet kitchen, and had promptly installed high-end double ovens.

She'd painted her walls a soft, warm peach color that reminded him of a woman's skin in the evening glow of a fireplace. A sofa and love seat were upholstered in a sand color reminiscent of the beach, and held throw pillows in soft pastels.

Photos dotted a side table under a painting of a seaside village. Pete had looked away quickly from the one of Melinda's parents. He didn't want to think about her mother, especially not at the moment.

"It must be the martinis because I can't believe I'm actually doing this," Mel said, tossing her hair over her naked shoulder and slipping first one beater, then the other, into their slots. Pete envied them, which was a little sick, but he couldn't help it.

"Why?" He stepped up behind her and cupped her bottom, stroking the smooth, warm skin revealed on either side of the thong. He squeezed it, then snugged his chin over her shoulder and got an intimate view of her bare breasts, which he took into his hands next. They filled his palms and spilled over, their shape and weight making him crazy; making him want to rip off her thong and bend her over the counter right then and there.

"Because I normally hide my body. I don't tart up and display it."

"And that's a damned shame, if you ask me." He himself wore nothing but a pair of boxers, and they weren't doing much to contain him. He pressed himself into her backside, groaning with the need to be inside her.

"I didn't." But Mel grinned as she plugged in her electric mixer and turned to kiss him over her shoulder. He pressed harder, and she shook it at him. "Wait for it, perv boy. Wait for it…"

Then she plunged the beaters into a steel bowl full of cream. He didn't know why he found the sight erotic, but he did.

"I can't," Pete told her.

She pushed back against him and wiggled, teasing him. "You don't have a choice." Then she turned on the mixer.

The noise should have been a mood-killer, but the small engine just served to remind him how hot his own was running, and as he stood behind her, playing with her breasts and watching the cream in the bowl slowly thicken, he imagined just what he'd do with it when it was ready.

And then, finally, it was.

That's when he took control of things. As soon as Melinda turned off the mixer, he unplugged it and took it away from her, ejecting the beaters into the sink. He turned her around, grabbed the bowl and a spoon and drew her down with him onto the kitchen rug.

"What about the melted chocolate?" she asked, laughing as he pushed her down flat.

"It goes by the wayside. I can't wait any longer, Mel. I really can't." He dipped the spoon into the whipped cream and slathered it all over her breasts.

"That's cold!" she protested.

He dropped a small gob onto her nose, for good measure. "Hey!"

Pete ignored her, popped the spoon into her mouth to silence her, and then flipped up her little 1950s housewife apron. He spread her knees and went to town with the whipped cream while she squirmed and laughed helplessly.

"Be still and behave," he ordered, "or I'll have to give you the spatula treatment."

"Promises, promises." Her eyes held amusement, desire and a sweet kind of trust that tugged at his heart. She could never, ever know about her mother's trip to Playa Bella to see him. He pushed that inappropriate, ill-timed thought away and got seriously down to having dessert.

MELINDA LAY SPRAWLED lazily on her kitchen rug, but all the lassitude left her body as Pete took one of her breasts into his mouth, getting a face-full of whipped cream as he did so. His teeth abraded her nipple, his tongue gently tortured it, and hot streaks of pleasure shot down to her core.

He laved every ounce of the cream from one breast before turning to the other, sucking and pulling on it, too. She stirred restlessly under him, her hips moving unconsciously, her body fully awakened and every nerve ending singing.

Her grandmother's apron was bunched up, wadded at her waist. She felt another flash of shame about wearing it in these circumstances, but that tinge of shame just made her feel hotter, naughtier, more free.

He worked his way down her stomach, kissing and licking. She forgot to suck in, simply because it felt so good. And then...

Oh, and then.

He eased her thighs further apart, slipped his hands under her backside, and brought her bliss. Just the sight of his dark head bent over her there was erotic. But the sensations he elicited as he went down were indescribably good.

She lifted herself to his mouth, writhing like a cat in heat, and couldn't have cared less. Embarrassment fell away, forgotten, and all that mattered was the rainbow he painted right at her center, the delicious tension ratcheting up and up until she burst into the chaotic color of her orgasm. She clutched at his shoulders, his head, while sounds she didn't recognize came from her own throat until she collapsed into a spent puddle of woman.

Pete lifted his head and grinned. "Much better than Insta-Wip," he said. "You sure as hell can't get that out of a can."

"Come here," she said weakly.

"Why, certainly, Mistress Mel."

"I want you inside me, right now."

"Thought you'd never ask." He was hard, his cock jutting out aggressively from his body, as if ready to go to war. He ditched his boxers and slid on top of her, levering himself up on his arms and looking down at her. "God, you're b—" he caught himself just in time, and she smiled "—hot."

He gave her an answering smile, kissed her, and eased into her body, igniting her all over again. He filled her, not only with his cock but with affection and laughter and confidence, and she couldn't help but respond on a level that went far beyond the physical.

He wanted her, despite the numbers on the scale. He wanted her, in violation of everything she'd been brought up to believe. He wanted her for who she was.

Melinda felt something far bigger than an orgasm building within her...it was a bubble of pure joy. She wanted to dance on a rooftop, to sing and shout her happiness—and yet, bizarrely, she also wanted to cry.

As her body built to yet another peak under his, a lump rose in her throat and tears pricked at her eyes. She and Pete came at the same time, something that had never happened for her before, rocking and shuddering.

Then she began to sob in his arms.

"What?" Pete was clearly alarmed. "Oh my God, did I hurt you?"

She shook her head.

"Honey, what is it? Tell me." He rolled them onto their sides, bodies still joined. "What's the matter? Hmm?"

"F-f-feel so good..." She buried her face in his shoulder.

"But then why—?"

"So used to f-feeling so bad around men..."

"Oh, baby. Come here, Mel." He held her tightly.

"Don't know what to d-do with this…"

"Shhhhh. You don't do anything with it, sweetheart. You just let it be. You just enjoy it. You feel good, okay? That's all."

She hesitated, then nodded.

He wiped her tears away with his thumbs, and she'd never felt so understood, so cherished.

She'd also never felt so afraid of her own vulnerability.

16

"So," PETE SAID, still ignoring his conscience as he moved inside Melinda again later as they lay on her bed. "I think you should come and work for Playa Bella."

"Mmm," was her immediate response, as she arched to meet his next thrust. Then, "What about your current pastry chef?"

"He's gone," Pete assured her, knowing that Reynaldo would make that true as soon as they'd secured Mel's services. He felt bad for the guy, but it wasn't his decision and it couldn't be helped in the face of Reynaldo's resolve.

"I thought you agreed not to do a sell job on me if I had a drink with you."

Pete grinned. "I didn't mention it at all while we were at The Blue Martini, did I?"

"You play dirty," she complained.

"I'm about to play dirtier," he promised, pulling out and then sliding down her body.

For the next few minutes, she had no more complaints—only accolades.

Afterward, he levered himself over her, putting his weight on his elbows, and smoothed the dark hair back from her forehead. He kissed her, long and tenderly. "So will you think about it? About coming to work at Playa Bella?"

She shook her head. "I like being independent, Pete. Having my own business. Calling the shots. I don't want to answer to anyone."

"You'd have a great salary, benefits, 401k…"

"Yeah, no. I just got out from under my overbearing parents four years ago. The last thing I need is an overbearing boss—especially one as chauvinist as that Reynaldo guy. Sorry."

Pete mulled over her answer. So she wanted independence. She didn't want a boss. How could he meet her terms and still get her on board for Reynaldo? How could he make everyone happy?

It was his area of expertise.

He could find a way to do it.

He knew he could. He always did.

He lay back down beside Melinda and took her hand as they lay together in the dark, with just a shimmer of moonlight sliding in through a gap in her bedroom curtains.

"What did you mean when you said the Green Machine was your escape chute?" she asked.

The question took him by surprise. "Why?"

"I don't know—your voice got funny when you said it."

He stayed silent.

"What did you want to escape from?"

Pete shifted uncomfortably. "My brother," he said after a pause. "My dad."

She waited expectantly.

"They didn't get along. My dad used to beat the crap out of my brother—he'd mouth off to him—and when it first started, I'd hide."

"Oh. That's awful."

"I was a lot younger," Pete said, hearing the defensiveness in his own voice. "I was scared."

Mel squeezed his hand.

"It would usually start with my dad yelling at my mom. He never hit her. He would hit the wall next to her head, or the door. But my mom would start to cry, and that would make my brother mad and so he'd say something, and then my dad would yell at him, but then go right back to yelling at my mom.

"So then my brother would get in his face and tell him to stop. And then my mom would scream at him to leave it alone, but it would be too late…my dad wouldn't let himself hit a woman, but he'd unload on Brent."

"Oh, Pete," Mel said. "I'm sorry. Everyone thought your dad was a nice guy. We had no idea."

He shrugged. "Of course you didn't. Nobody did. Brent was years older than us. Brent would go get in fights at school, too, so that he didn't get asked by teachers about the bruises. I thought he was just crazy, but he sort of knew what he was doing, in a sick way. He didn't want child protective services on our doorstep."

Mel put a hand up to his cheek.

"I used to crawl under the bed," Pete continued. "Then came the day when my brother pulled me out by the ankle and started punching me, you know, afterward. He had a split lip and this nasty expression on his face and he told me to shut up and stop crying. That he wasn't going to cry, and that I couldn't, either."

"My parents heard us fighting and then my dad came in and it was even worse for Brent. They were crashing around the room. The window was open, so I pushed out the screen and dropped to the ground outside and ran.

"The pattern was kind of set that day. It went on like that for years, but I was home as little as possible. I went to friends' houses, I worked my paper route, I played sports, I worked on my car. I wasn't your typical rebel second child. I was the good kid. Brent smoked pot, called me a pussy, dropped out of high school and worked in a restaurant. He ended up joining the army at age nineteen. I kept my mouth shut, avoided conflict, got good grades and went to college."

"I'm sorry," Mel said again.

"If my parents got into a fight," Pete mused, "I just told myself that he never actually hit her, and so it was okay. I ignored it. I didn't want to be his stand-in punching bag, you know?

"He grabbed me once and shook me like a terrier shakes a rat. He was screaming, 'Take a shot at me! Take a punch! Go ahead, you little shit! I know you want to!'" And I couldn't. I just closed my eyes and basically played dead until he dropped me to the ground. I was a pussy—to him, anyway. But not on the football field."

"You were not," Melinda said. "And that's an ugly word, anyway. You were smart, Pete. You refused to engage with a crazy person, an abusive jerk."

He rolled away from her to face the wall. "Smart? I don't know about that. I just followed old habit. I didn't want my teeth on the floor in a pool of blood, like my brother's."

"You did the right thing," Mel said. After a pause, she asked, "What happened with your parents? I heard they moved to Birmingham, but…is your mom okay?"

Pete nodded and rolled back to face her. "My mom is great. You know what happened? Brent was gone and I was in college when my dad finally really hurt himself—he punched a stud, broke his hand, and she had to take him to the hospital. She left his ass in the waiting room and told him to get counseling for his temper. That the marriage was over."

"So did he?"

"Yep. When he got home with his hand in a cast there was

a cold casserole waiting with a note that said she'd gone to her mother's. She'd be back home again when he'd gone to see a therapist for six months and had the bills to prove it. So I guess after a couple of months of relying on ESPN and sit-coms for company and being utterly domestically challenged, he did. Then he went through an anger management class and now he waits patiently while she yells at him on occasion."

Mel laughed. "You're kidding."

Pete shook his head. "Nope. I'm not. I almost fell over in shock the day I saw it for myself."

"Well, good for her!"

"She tried to make him apologize to my brother, too. But that didn't fly—my brother can antagonize the old man with a glance."

"I didn't know Brent well," Melinda said thoughtfully, "but he always seemed angry about something. He always had an attitude."

"Born that way," Pete said. "Chipped his shoulder com-ing out of the womb, had colic as a baby and never got over the bellyaching. Then again, I don't think either of my par-ents was ready to have kids when they did. They were too young. My dad didn't want to share my mom with 'the brat.' Nice, huh?"

"Then it's actually amazing that they're still together."

"That's one word for it."

"Do you wish they weren't?"

Pete didn't know how to answer that. "I used to wish my mom would leave him," he said. "I was terrified of him. Now he just seems like a fat, middle-aged grocery sack that I don't relate to, much. But I guess she'd be lonely without him."

IT WAS LATER, after they'd been asleep for hours, that Pete woke up feeling horribly guilty. He'd accepted Jocelyn Edgeworth's business, asked out her daughter as required, had made love

to her and was even now plotting to manipulate her into his boss's web at Playa Bella. He was the shit in a Machiavellian sandwich.

Unfortunately, he'd also woken up with the perfect idea: the one that would make everyone, including himself, happy.

Reynaldo had told him to find a solution for the boutique's retail space. Reynaldo had told him to hire Mel. But Mel wanted independence; her own shop.

So why not open a boutique bakery, right there in Playa Bella's retail space? The more he thought about the idea, the more he liked it. Mel would get increased traffic from the hotel, and could raise her prices because of the elegant surroundings. The hotel made money from leasing the space, and could benefit even more from Mel being there if they somehow showcased her.

"A holiday baking open house," he said aloud, not even realizing it. "A gingerbread house competition, with the elaborate entries auctioned off for charity at a big ball. Better yet, she offers baking and cake-decorating classes. Or...she has her own televised show!"

"Whah?" Mel murmured sleepily.

"Yes!" Pete shouted, smacking his hand down on the mattress and forgetting all about guilt and Machiavelli.

"Aaaaagh!" Melinda bolted upright, her hair wildly askew and her naked breasts bouncing. "What? What's wrong?"

Unable to help himself, Pete tweaked a nipple. "Playa Bella will have our very own Ace of Cakes!"

Mel yelped, smacking his hand in the dark. "What are you talking about? Why would your hotel feature a TV show about baking?" She almost knocked her bedside lamp over as she reached for the switch.

"I'm brilliant," Pete announced, as the room became illuminated.

"That's nice. Why aren't you asleep and brilliant?" she asked, a little acidly.

"No, really! We showcase you, feature you, make you a star!"

"Pete, do you have a fever? Have you been drinking?"

"Listen," he ordered, and told her of his vision. "We have to do something different with that retail space anyway—it can't stay in business trying to sell three-hundred dollar ties the color of a flamingo's butt—"

"You're crazy," Mel said.

"No! This can work, I promise you."

"I have an existing lease," she protested. "I built out the space. I bought commercial ovens and equipment—"

"All of which can be moved," he pointed out. "And I bet I can sweet-talk you out of the lease or offer the owner something in return...I'm really good at that."

"I'm sure you are, but what makes you think I want to move onto the premises of Playa Bella? It will change the whole nature of my business."

"Your business will explode," Pete told her. "Just think about it."

"I am thinking about it," Mel said in dubious tones. "And I'm not sure I want to teach classes—"

"Why not, if it will bring you more customers?"

"—not to mention that there's no way you can guarantee me a TV show, Pete. You're not God!"

"No, that's true, but Reynaldo just happens to be a big stockholder in the WMIA affiliate's parent corporation, and it would only be a good thing for him and Playa Bella if we wrote a pilot and pitched it. Or we can start with a small local cable show. You don't understand, sweetheart—this could be a huge moneymaker for everyone involved, and bring an enormous customer base right to our doorstep. Then you could come out with a line of cookie cutters and bake pans

in the shapes you mentioned at Mark's wedding—starfish, sand dollars, boats, fish, suns…"

Mel muttered something that sounded like "that'd show Gutierrez." She began to look thoughtful, and Pete knew he had her.

Then her expression changed. "But I'd have to work for that creep, Reynaldo."

"No, no, no. You'd be your own boss."

"But within his hotel, which means that he ultimately calls the shots," she said, balking.

"Nope. You'd just be leasing the space, like you do right now at your current shop. You build it out the way you want to and bring in the equipment. Easy. You don't answer to Reynaldo. You'd barely see the man. And," Pete added, unable to resist, "you could still get those free massages at the Playa Bella spa." He grinned.

She squinted at him in the lamplight, chewing on her bottom lip.

"Hey, stop that. You'll eat it right off. Only I'm allowed to chew on your lip," he teased.

"Getting awfully bossy and proprietary, aren't you?"

"Why? Are there other men you allow to chew it?" Pete asked, getting unexpectedly cranky about the idea.

"Maybe not exactly…"

He rolled onto her naked body and mock glowered down at her. "Not exactly? What do you let other men do to you?"

"I don't know. Things I like them to do," she bluffed.

"Things like this?" He took one of her breasts into his mouth and pleasured it.

Mel moaned. "Huh-uh."

"Then how about this?" He did similar things to her other breast.

"No," she said, gasping a little.

Pete slid down south, way south, and did something wicked.

"Oh, Pete," she sighed. "No other guy does that either, so please don't stop…"

17

"AND SO," PETE FINISHED, his arms spread wide, "this is a fantastic solution for us all, don't you agree, sir?" He aimed a toothy grin at his boss.

They sat in Reynaldo's office with its sweeping views of the bay and downtown Miami. A life-size portrait of the man in polo garb, standing next to a massive bay thoroughbred, loomed from the opposite wall. A bronze bust of Reynaldo crowned its own mahogany pedestal. And Reynaldo's latest tousled-haired trophy wife, dripping with diamonds, gazed triumphantly at visitors from an eight-by-ten-inch, gilt-framed photo on a desk so large it rated its own zip code.

"Not to mention that the Have a Heart Foundation has scheduled their ball here at Playa Bella in mid-October, and the Charity League Holiday Bazaar will be here in December. Projected revenues are up by...drumroll...twenty-two percent."

And if those projected figures turned into solid ones by year's end, Pete's future at Reynaldo hotels was assured.

"Hmm," Reynaldo said, rolling a Cuban cigar between his palms. "A boutique bakery?" He frowned. "You'll have to check with the health department—I think she will have

to do her baking in the existing kitchens, though she could sell the goods in the storefront."

Pete thought about this. Melinda wouldn't like it. She preferred having her own small, private domain.

"And we would receive a percentage of sales under the arrangement, eh, Pedro?"

Pete had no idea if this was okay with Mel, but he nodded. He'd take it up with her—and his annoying conscience—later.

Reynaldo was now flipping the cigar from end to end between his index fingers and thumbs. "If she is using the Playa Bella kitchens, however, then I see no reason to have a separate pastry chef. She should do our commercial baking here, as well."

"Whoa, whoa, whoa..." Pete held up a hand, but in the face of Reynaldo's raised, supercilious eyebrows, he dropped it. "I doubt she'll agree, sir."

"I see no reason to underwrite her expenses and publicity if she is not contributing to our bottom line." Reynaldo clamped the Cuban between his teeth and folded his arms across his chest.

"I think she'll contribute a great deal to our bottom line, sir. Especially if she brings in the kind of traffic I've projected, and puts Playa Bella in the spotlight as a culinary destination. I'm envisioning a multi-week gourmet baking course with a dessert-wine tasting, eventually. And it could be international, especially with your great contacts in Columbia, Venezuela and Argentina. If you can get some of those jet-setters down there to come up and play golf while their wives—"

"Please." Reynaldo waved a hand. "Those people have paid chefs on staff," he said dismissively. "Their wives don't cook."

"We appeal to their artistic sensibilities," Pete said. "This

isn't cooking. It's high art that only the most sophisticated and elegant can appreciate…much less achieve."

Reynaldo cast his eyes heavenward.

"Besides, there's also the spa for these ladies, as you have so astutely pointed out. And high-end shopping nearby at Bal Harbour, Merrick Park Mall, Miracle Mile."

His boss pursed his thick lips around the Cuban.

"There are very fine gentlemen's establishments for the men," Pete continued, "not to mention exclusive private gambling a mere limo's ride away. We make it a couples' destination vacation, with plenty of options."

Reynaldo grunted. "I still say the girl takes over as pastry chef as well, or there is too much expense with too much risk."

Pete looked at him in dismay. Mel would never agree… unless?

"I don't think we ultimately want her focus there, sir. But maybe she could have a sous-chef under her direction who handles that aspect? You could pay the sous-chef less than half what you'd have to pay Melinda. And this way, if she comes on board, she pays you for the retail space and you don't pay her a dime. She brings in notoriety plus revenue, and you get an added percentage of that. Where's the downside?"

His boss chomped on the cigar thoughtfully.

"So you end up saving—" Pete figured out the number and told him.

"I like it," Reynaldo said finally. "Okay. Make it happen, Pedro. Start low, though, with a basic job offer. Can't hurt. I give you full authority to negotiate for me. Get a contract together. See it through."

And just like that, they were off and running.

Pete couldn't wait to tell Melinda.

Then he remembered the Machiavellian sandwich. What the hell was he doing?

Nothing wrong, he told himself. He was truly doing only what was best for everybody. He was keeping Reynaldo and Jocelyn and himself and Melinda all happy. It was a win-win-win-win situation.

THINGS BEGAN BADLY for Pete when he started, as per the Big R's instructions, with a general job offer, not so generous salary and bare-bones benefits.

"No," Melinda said simply. "Not interested."

Pete upped the salary, keeping everything else the same.

"Nope. I told you, I don't want to work for anyone but myself."

He nodded. "Okay, then. I'm authorized to offer you the boutique on a lease…" He made her an offer that he found fair but was still very favorable to Playa Bella.

Mel's eyes flashed blue fire. She raised her chin and shook her head. "That's a high rent to begin with, Pete, and there's no way I'm giving away fifteen percent of my sales to that little Latin Caesar."

Pete spread his hands wide, palms up. "The rent is incredibly reasonable for the luxury space and high-end amenities you get in return. Plus the new, up-market clientele. And free parking."

"I have free parking now. The space isn't any larger than what I have here, and the only true 'amenity' I can think of is carpet, which I don't want. And what's wrong with my middle-class clientele? They keep my doors open just as well as snooty ladies with Dior doggie-carriers." No need to tell Pete that she was worried about how to pay expenses after losing the Java Joe's account. She'd just keep that to herself.

"So what would you find more reasonable?" Pete asked. "Name your figure."

First player to throw out a number loses. "Name yours."

Mel gave him a lipless social smile straight out of her mother's repertoire and enjoyed watching him squirm.

Pete dragged a hand down his face. "Listen, I'd love to give it to you for free, darlin', I hope you know that—"

"Of course." She brightened her smile and didn't give him an inch. She had a business to run.

"—but I negotiate on behalf of Reynaldo."

"Exactly."

Pete sighed. "Okay, how about the monthly lease and twelve percent of profits? Remember, he'll pay for the build-out—"

"Big of him, since he can keep it the same and throw a coffee shop into the space later."

"—and get you on your own cable show—"

"Which is time-consuming, takes my attention away from work, and has a small, limited, local audience."

"—as well as provide a sous-chef to handle your responsibilities here at Playa Bella—"

"Responsibilities which I don't want, not to mention the fact that he'll save money by hiring a sous-chef and just putting my name on the menu."

Pete's pleasant smile was fraying at the edges. "But you're getting a phenomenal opportunity with us."

Mel sat back, increasing the distance between them, while Pete still leaned forward. "You came to me," she pointed out.

He gave a slight nod to acknowledge this.

"So make it worth my while. Just because I'm a girl—" here she got in a jab at Reynaldo "—does not mean that I'm naïve or that all I think about is my nails."

"Of course not. You're a very astute businesswoman." Pete tossed out his true offer, the one he was not prepared to go below. "All right. The monthly lease money and ten percent of the profits. Your name on the menu but no actual responsibility besides designing the dessert menu and providing

the recipes to the sous-chef. The cable show, seasonal baking contests sponsored and promoted by Playa Bella. That's an unbelievable deal."

"An offer I can't refuse?"

Pete nodded, expecting to wrap this up.

Melinda pursed her lips. "Take five hundred bucks off the monthly rent and Playa Bella gets two percent of the profits."

Pete's jaw dropped open. "You're smoking crack," he said as pleasantly as it was possible to say such a thing. "A hundred bucks off the rent and eight percent."

By the time she'd finished with him, he looked downtrodden, rumpled and frustrated. But Mel was exultant. She'd shaved three hundred bucks off the monthly lease amount and chiseled him down to three and a half percent of her sales.

Pete glared at her, shoved his hands into his pockets and headed for the door. "I'll have our attorneys draw up the papers."

"Don't I get a kiss?" Mel asked, innocently.

"I don't kiss sharks," he growled.

"Aw. I'm just a furry wittle bunny wabbit, I swear." Melinda batted her eyelashes at him.

He glowered at her. "Pickpocket bunny with fangs."

Melinda laughed.

He didn't.

"It was your idea, you know," she called after him as he pushed open the door of her shop.

"Don't remind me."

"Hey! You forgot your free cookie!"

Slam.

"Poor thing," Melinda said to Mami as she skipped into her office. "He must have a headache."

Mami wagged her tail. Then she yawned, entirely unconcerned.

PETE'S WEEK DIDN'T get much better.

Even though he invented a piranha of an attorney, a six-foot-five ex-boxer, to blame for the lousy deal with Melinda, Reynaldo wasn't pleased that he'd been bested by a girl and insinuated that he'd lost both his mind and his shriveled *gringo* balls during the encounter. As a reward, Pete had to fire the existing pastry chef in person, on the slimmest of pretexts.

He felt horrible, as the man first exhibited shock, then pleaded abjectly for his job and finally went into a violent frenzy, knocking pans and baking supplies off the shelves as he exited.

Pete spent a moment standing in the silent, aghast kitchen, head bent forward, the bridge of his nose pinched between his thumb and forefinger. Then he got a broom and cleaned up the mess.

He'd brushed the flour off his pant legs and the ground hazelnuts out of his wing tips. He'd gone upstairs and was running numbers in his office when the concierge desk buzzed him to say that Mrs. Jocelyn Edgeworth was downstairs to see him.

"Oh, farg me," Pete said aloud.

"*Perdón?*" Tomas, the concierge, was from Ecuador.

"Nothing. Send her up. Thank you."

"Farging" Pete turned out to be precisely what Jocelyn had in mind, though not literally.

"Darling Peter," she said as she swept into his office in a pale pink checked pantsuit and pink patent-leather Mary Janes, "don't be ridiculous."

Pete raised his weary gaze to meet her expertly made up, vicious baby-blues. "Excuse me?"

She removed two fat manila envelopes from her Gucci tote and shook them at him. "There must be some mistake."

Pete stretched his lips into the semblance of a smile. "I

don't think so. I went over the agreements myself. The date for the Have a Heart Foundation ball is October 23, the Charity League Holiday Bazaar is on December 2, and we've cleared January 17 for the Every Breath You Take lung cancer fundraiser."

"I'm not concerned with the dates, Peter. I'm talking about the charges. Where are my discounts?"

"Discounts, Mrs. Edgeworth?"

"Pee-ter. I've brought you not one, not two, but three big charity events and I expect some serious consideration for such."

He gave it consideration. He considered making her eat the bronze Longhorn on his desk, slowly, with her pinkies elevated. Then he considered forcing her to sit on it, instead.

"Mrs. Edgeworth, I really don't have the authority to discount—"

"That's just nonsense. You know it and I know it."

Pete gritted his teeth. It was nonsense, but most people had the courtesy to play the game with him and then fawn all over him when he made a "special exception" for them, one that he "really shouldn't" make.

"Take thirty percent of the ballroom rentals right off the top, for starters," she demanded.

Pete's throat swelled in outrage. "That's impossible. I can't do that, Mrs. Edgeworth."

"Why not?" Her eyes held all the warmth of titanium bores, and were just as deadly.

"Because your events are on Saturdays during the high season! I've already given you a good rate. The best I can do on top of that is give you five percent off the rentals."

"Pee-ter. These events are for char-i-ty. You don't pillage the coffers of charities. You contribute to them. You act with goodwill."

"I'm not pillaging your charities, Mrs. E. We have a busi-

ness to run, here at Playa Bella. I'm sorry, but five-percent off is the best I can do. Your guests purchase expensive tickets and tables, big booths at the bazaar. And you run a silent auction. That's how you raise the funds."

"Fine. Then donate the liquor," she said.

"I can't do that—you know it would amount to thousands of dollars!"

"The food, then."

"Not going to hap—"

"The desserts!"

"Why don't you ask your daughter to donate the desserts? She'll be opening a bakery boutique in our retail space."

Silence shrieked between them for a few moments.

Tension.

Then Jocelyn's aristocratic nostrils flared.

"Why don't I ask my daughter about her new beau?" she suggested, smacking the manila envelopes down loudly in the middle of his desk. She shot him that lipless cobra smile of hers.

He met her gaze evenly. "Are you threatening me, Mrs. Edgeworth?"

"Peter, darling." She waved a languid hand. "I'd never do something so inelegant."

Pete's head was going to explode, it really was. He could feel the rocket fuel gathering at the back of his neck, turning into a tight ball of rage. It was spreading across his shoulders, too.

He sucked in a deep breath and forced himself to lay his hands flat on his desk, so that they couldn't curl into fists. *She won't do it. It would hurt her daughter too much. She's bluffing.*

Jocelyn drummed her fingernails against the leather of her Gucci tote. "But I could certainly check with the Standard and

the Ritz and even the Delano to see if they have ballrooms available on these dates."

The bottom line was that he didn't want to lose the business, however much he'd like to toss her and her Italian leather tote off the roof.

Pete dredged up the last courteous smile he could muster and forced it onto his lips. "Of course you're free to do that, Mrs. Edgeworth," he said. "Meanwhile, why don't I discuss this matter of a discount with Mr. Reynaldo and get back to you?"

"Why, Peter." She summoned her bloodless smirk again. "That would be lovely." She curled two fingers in to her palm in a sign that for him would always signify the Texas Longhorns. But she turned it sideways and held an imaginary phone to her ear. "Call me."

18

"YOU MUST BE JOKING, Pedro." Reynaldo ran his manicured fingers over the bronze bust of himself in his office, removing imaginary dust particles from its stylized locks of hair.

Pete tried not to think about how much he despised being called Pedro. "No, sir. Jocelyn Edgeworth wants a thirty percent discount on her gigs, or she'll look into moving them to the Standard, the Ritz or the Delano."

Reynaldo muttered something in Spanish. Pete was pretty sure it translated into something like "socialite whore."

"I don't like being badgered, and especially not by a woman. Has her daughter signed the contracts for the boutique bakery yet?"

"I'm meeting with Melinda on Wednesday to do that."

"Good." Reynaldo went to his elaborate humidor and chose yet another of his vast array of Cuban cigars. "First, preempt the mother. Call and reserve the big ballrooms at those hotels for the relevant dates, if they're available. Use my wife's mother's name. And call any other suitable venues, as well."

Pete's eyebrows shot up to his hairline. "But they'll want credit-card numbers."

"Give them my alternate Am Ex Black Card number." His

boss gave him a crocodile smile around the cigar. "I'll cancel it next week."

"The charges will still—"

"I assure you that I am a very good customer. One that they will not wish to offend. And I will not know how those charges got onto my card. Clearly the number was stolen, eh?"

Pete blinked.

"A vengeful employee or girlfriend. After all, why would I make all of those reservations for the same date? It makes no sense."

"O-kay."

"Stall the mother until you get the contracts signed with the daughter. Then tell the mother that I won't even authorize a five-percent discount, unless…" Reynaldo added something incredibly crude in Spanish and laughed as he sat down in his rolling leather chair, knees spread wide.

Pete stared at him. Had his boss really suggested that Jocelyn could negotiate further on her knees and under his desk?

Granted, he'd developed quite a dislike for the woman, but that was going too far. She was his girlfriend's mother, after all. And though he despised the way she'd gone about it, he couldn't really blame her for trying to get a better deal.

"Next," Reynaldo said, "you mention to her that she would not want to jeopardize her daughter's arrangement with us, eh?"

A strangled noise escaped Pete's throat; he couldn't hold it back. This was like dancing naked, dangling his meat over a standoff between a cobra and a rattlesnake. Would Jocelyn and Reynaldo strike each other? Or the nearest conveniently placed object?

"She will have no choice but to hold her events here at Playa Bella," Reynaldo said complacently, snipping the tip off his cigar with a platinum cutter. "And as for the daughter, make sure that my standard escape clause is in her contracts, eh? If she gets difficult, she can blow me, too."

Pete literally saw red at the words. His first impulse was to reach across the desk and seize his boss by the neck, pull him out of his chair and stomp on his face.

But he made himself count to three. He reminded himself that he was not his father. That there was a lot at stake, here, and more than his own job: Melinda's future. He'd already helped break her existing lease, and she'd posted the news in her shop.

Reynaldo squinted at him through a curl of cigar smoke. "You are still here, Pedro. Why is that? Is there something further that we need to discuss?"

Pete swallowed. He opened his mouth to say it. *Melinda is my girlfriend, you rat bastard, so disrespect her again and I will knock your teeth down your throat.*

But again, he reminded himself: it wasn't only his career that was at stake here, now. It was hers. And the economy was horrendous.

Keep your mouth closed, man. Just shut the hell up.

"Ah. How could I have forgotten, Pedro?" His boss got to his feet and crossed the room once again to his humidor.

Don't call me Pedro, you son of a bitch.

"Your revenues—assuming we keep Mrs. Edgeworth's charity events here—have risen the required twenty percent. So, welcome to the executive team here at Playa Bella. You are the new vice president of business development."

And Reynaldo tossed Pete a top of the line Monte Cristo.

He wanted to let it drop to the floor. He wanted to step on it. But Pete caught it. "Thank you, sir."

"Call me Rafi," Reynaldo said.

Pete set his jaw. "Thanks, Rafi."

PETE MADE THE CALLS to other hotels, giving out "Rafi's" alternate Black Card number with abandon. After all, Joce-

lyn was the one who'd started playing dirty pool, and so his conscience didn't really bother him—much.

But when it came time to sign copies of Mel's contract at the lawyer's office, he balked, wishing that the ex-boxer, the piranha attorney he'd dreamed up, really existed. Pete knew damned well that Reynaldo's invidious "escape" clause was in every legal document his lawyers produced.

"Melinda, you may want to have your own attorney look over the contract before you sign it," he suggested over lunch the day before.

But Mel, his little pickpocket bunny, seemed to have retracted her fangs. She aimed a sunny smile at him. "Oh, Pete. Don't be silly—you've read it, right?"

He nodded. What else could he do?

"Well, I trust you completely. Why should I waste hundreds of dollars on another legal opinion?"

Because I work for an immoral asshole. Pete finally got what his friend Dev was all about. Dev's morals were somewhat...elastic. But he did have a complete set of them, despite his jokes to the contrary. Dev played pranks.

Reynaldo, on the other hand, genuinely screwed people for fun—on impulse, and just because he could. Rafi was the very definition of immoral. He'd never met a business or marriage vow he hadn't broken. In fact, he seemed to find such things amusing.

And the more Pete's eyes opened to the truth, the less he wanted Melinda to have anything to do with Reynaldo and Playa Bella. But since he'd brought her in on a platter, how could he tell her that?

"I just think it makes good business sense to always have your own lawyer," Pete said.

"Agreed. But not necessary in this case." Mel reached across the table and squeezed his hand. "Thanks, though. I appreciate you being so up-front."

Pete groaned inwardly.

"You'll come with me to the attorney's office, right? And we can go celebrate the contract afterward."

"Sure."

THE ATTORNEY'S OFFICES were in a big white bank building on Brickell, and they sat at a long conference table, attended by a busy paralegal.

"Here you are," she said, pushing three copies of the contract towards Melinda. "Mr. Reynaldo sends his apologies for being unable to attend the meeting. He's already signed the papers, as you can see. Now you sign, Ms. Edgeworth, where the yellow markers are."

It was now or never. Pete swiped the pen that the paralegal held out to Mel. "This is a black pen. Ms. Edgeworth prefers to sign original documents in blue."

Mel stared at him. "I do?"

"Yes," Pete said decisively. He turned to the paralegal. "Do you mind getting another?"

"Sure." The woman left the room.

Pete darted after her and locked the door. "Mel," he whispered. "Look at the second to last page. Find the termination clause. Strike it out and initial it. Do the same with the two other copies."

"What are you talking about?"

"Melinda, just do it. Now."

The doorknob jiggled as the paralegal tried to get back into the room. Pete strode to the door, opened it but blocked the entrance with his body, and slid out, closing it behind him.

"Ms. Edgeworth is on an unexpected emergency call," she heard him say on from the corridor. "She needs a moment or two of privacy."

"Oh. Uh. Okay," the paralegal stammered. "But I'm required by law to witness her signatures."

"No problem. She'll be off the line in a minute. Thanks so much for your patience."

Melinda flipped quickly through the documents and isolated the clause he'd indicated. It was in dense legalese, and seemed innocuous. But she struck through the paragraphs with the black pen, and then quickly initialed the margins next to them. That page, she noted with relief, did not require a signature.

She smoothed the documents and pulled her cell phone from her purse, placing it on the table. Then she got up, walked to the door and turned the knob. "Thank you," she said warmly to the paralegal. "I appreciate the privacy. Sorry about that."

The woman came back into the room, seemed to find nothing amiss, and Mel calmly signed the contracts with the newly provided blue pen. She put her copy into her purse, shook hands with the paralegal and thanked her again.

Pete and Melinda walked out of the plush legal offices and rode down the elevator in silence. They emerged from the building into the torpid September air.

"What was that all about?" Melinda asked.

"Saving your bacon," Pete said.

"And why did my bacon need to be saved, exactly?" Her blue eyes were as serious as Pete had ever seen them.

He sighed. "Because you didn't get a lawyer of your own and I felt obligated, even though my loyalty should be to my company, and not to the sheep my boss likes to fleece."

"Stop talking about bacon and mutton and speak English, Pete. This isn't a barnyard."

"No, it's a jungle," he retorted. "Mel, you're one hell of a negotiator, but don't ever, ever, sign a contract again without having a trained legal professional look at it."

"I thought I could trust you!"

"Looks like you were right." He dragged his hands down his face. "Not that I feel very good about it."

She put her hands on her hips. "I don't understand you."

"Good. That makes two of us. Now, where do you want to go to celebrate our mutual confusion and your contract?"

They went to Segofredo and ordered champagne cocktails, which Pete regretted immediately because of the sweetness. After a toast, he pushed his aside and ordered a dirty martini. He knew it was going to be a long night.

Melinda took a couple of moments to call Kylie, her aunt, from the bar and tell her the good news. Then she dialed part of another number, but stopped.

"What's wrong? Who were you going to call?"

"My parents," she said, looking suddenly miserable. "But I don't even want to talk to my mother."

That makes two of us, sweetheart. Pete made a sympathetic noise.

"She'd only find a way to insult me, somehow, and ruin the moment. I don't want to go there." Mel sighed. "I hate not speaking to her, but I hate speaking to her even more. Does that make any sense?"

He nodded. "Can you call your dad's cell phone?"

Mel rolled her champagne glass between her palms. "No. My mother would be insulted, and we'd start a whole new Cold War."

"So tell them in a couple of days."

She nodded. "And Mark's busy with the legislative session up in Tallahassee, so I'll tell him when he gets back."

Within a few minutes, her excitement bubbled up again.

Pete loved the animation in her expression and the sparkle in her eyes. He was happy for her—this was a good deal for her—but he still felt disloyal to his company. Then again, did a man like Reynaldo deserve loyalty?

Seeming to sense his misgivings, Melinda turned serious

again. She took a bracing sip of her drink and then eyed him warily. "Pete, are you saying that Reynaldo is going to try to screw me in our business dealings? What was that clause, exactly?"

He stabbed at the olives in his martini with a toothpick. "I'm not saying that. What I'm trying to tell you is that he… he normally reserves the right to screw people in his contracts. You know, in case they try to screw him first," he added lamely.

"Uh-huh."

"It's only smart business practice," he continued. Was it the words or the martini that left such a bad taste in his mouth?

"What I did in there—in the lawyer's office—was that even legal?"

He shrugged. "Sure it was. You struck out the clause before you signed, right? So what you did was just as legal as him burying the clause in the contract to begin with."

"But the paralegal didn't see me do it."

"That's her fault, not yours. She left the room. Then she didn't review the document again after you signed it."

"But you set her up. I don't like this, Pete."

"Can we just forget it?"

Melinda shook her head. "No. But I can say thank you." She slid off her bar stool and wedged herself between his open knees. She took his face in her hands and kissed him.

That was when Pete knew he'd done the right thing, even if it had felt incredibly wrong. Her gratitude, her trust, her love—they all meant a lot more to him than Playa Bella's bottom line.

Love?

Really?

Did Melinda love him? Did he love her? The word was a bit extreme. Pete shied away from it. All he knew for right now was that kissing her felt really good.

19

A WEEK LATER, Pete braced himself for the worst.

Melinda's Mommie Dearest did her cobra dance again, bobbing her head menacingly and giving him that lipless grimace of hers. Today she wore a snug spring-green suit that looked a half size too large in the jacket, giving her plenty of room to hyperventilate.

The woman still had phenomenal legs. Her narrow feet were encased in beige leather pumps with dagger heels. And today she carried a bag with little L's and V's all over it. As she began her rant, Pete idly calculated what she must spend yearly on handbags alone. It probably equaled, in dollar value, the gross national product of a third world country.

"I find it deeply suspicious, Pee-ter, that every decent hotel in Miami and South Beach is booked solid on the days of my charity events."

"Do you, Mrs. Edgeworth?"

"Yes."

"South Florida is very active during the high season. It's a top destination for wealthy travelers, ma'am."

"Don't lecture me like the Tourism Bureau, Peter."

"Wouldn't dream of it. Incidentally, I did discuss the matter of deep discounts for your events with Mr. Reynaldo. Un-

fortunately, we are unable to accommodate you at any less than full price."

"That's outrageous!"

"I'm sorry you feel that way, Mrs. E."

"Don't force me to have a serious talk with my daughter, young man."

"About that, Jocelyn—"

She bristled at his use of her first name.

"—are you aware that your daughter is working with Reynaldo to bring a boutique bakery here? And that she'll have her own cable TV show anchored from it?"

She froze, giving no reaction except for a long, slow blink. "I haven't spoken with my daughter in weeks."

"Mr. Reynaldo would hate for a deteriorating relationship with you yourself to jeopardize such a deal with your daughter, since it's very much to her benefit. It will make her a local celebrity and spotlight her business."

Score. Jocelyn actually gasped, and he was low enough to enjoy her shock and white rage. Whatever had happened to Peter S. Dale, CEO of Mr. Nice Guy, Inc.? Pete wasn't sure, but he didn't really care for this new man who'd taken his place.

"You bastard." Her hands shook with suppressed emotion. She reached into her purse and he had the wild thought that perhaps she had a concealed carry permit and was hunting for a gun. But she retrieved a handful of keys, to his relief. "You actually dare to use my daughter and her happiness against me?"

Pete leaned a hip against his desk and stared her down. "Didn't you do the very same thing? Turnabout is fair play, Mrs. E."

"I bribed you!" she exclaimed. "You're blackmailing me. That's different. Worse. Much worse."

"Is it?"

"You. Are. Going. To. Pay. Peter. Start wondering when the other shoe will drop."

He nodded. "How like you. Now that you're not getting your way, you'll hurt your daughter to exact revenge. You must enjoy being you, Jocelyn."

"At least," she spat, "I'm not using her, stringing her along, all the while planning to destroy her when she learns the truth."

"What exactly is the truth, Mrs. E? And why is it so damaging? I think your daughter is an amazing, beautiful, creative, smart, hardworking woman. I love spending time with her. I love going to bed with her. Shit, if she didn't come prepackaged with a mother-in-law like you, I'd probably propose to her!"

"Over my dead body," Jocelyn hissed, and stormed toward the door.

"Go stand in front of my car, woman," Pete growled. "It's the pale blue BMW Z-4 in the parking lot. Go stand in front of my car as I hit the gas, and I'll marry Melinda tomorrow."

SIX WEEKS LATER, an architect had drawn up preliminary plans for Melinda's boutique bakery in Playa Bella. She was naked in Pete's bed, and was, in fact, bound by the wrists to Pete's headboard with one hellaciously ugly pink necktie and one dark red power tie.

She still wasn't altogether sure how she'd gotten that way. He'd been stealthy and kept her laughing the whole time while distracting her with his clever mouth.

Her helpless position made her self-conscious. While she had relaxed a lot around Pete, something about being fully exposed and unable to cover herself made her feel bigger... and almost desperate. But she didn't want to reveal her psyche any more than she did her large thighs.

"You have to let me go," she insisted, casting about for a reason.

"Why?" He grinned at her with purely male enjoyment.

"So that I can show you the designs."

Pete waggled his eyebrows and bit her lightly on the thigh. "But I have designs of my own, and they involve keeping you right here on this mattress."

"Pete!" She tried not to let her distress show.

"I still haven't paid you back in full for jerking me around on the deal," he announced.

"I didn't jerk you around. I drove a hard bargain."

"Yep. And I intend to drive you with something hard, too." He grinned evilly.

"Uh-oh…but didn't we just do that?"

"Yes, my pretty Melinda, but now you've really got it coming. Uh, no pun intended." Pete got up and strolled, sans clothing, into his small galley kitchen.

She pulled futilely at the ties that bound her wrists, but couldn't help being distracted by his taut, muscular buns. Then she went back to tugging.

Stop it. Either you trust Pete, or you don't.

Did she trust him? Could she?

Were they having fun together, or was he having fun at her expense?

You let yourself be used, Melinda. Her mother's voice came back to haunt her. Was she still letting herself be used?

She heard the refrigerator door open and shut. Then fiendish male laughter, which did nothing to reassure her.

Pete came back and stood in front of her with something profane in his right hand. Something that was not in her culinary vocabulary. Something she did not recognize, and refused to recognize, as food.

Insta-Wip.

"No," she said.

"Oh, yeah, baby." Pete's smirk widened as he popped off the blue plastic top and shook the can with menace.

"You are not putting that on my body."

"That so?" He advanced upon her.

"No!" Melinda struggled against the ties restraining her. "I knew I should never have let you do this. I knew it!"

"Mwah ha ha ha…"

Pete was definitely having fun at her expense. So why was she laughing, too?

Mel shrieked as the first obscene whispering sound came from the can. *Shhhhhhhhhh!* And fake whipped cream, made with horrifying things like high-fructose corn syrup, partially hydrogenated oils, and cheap man-made chemicals, hit her skin.

Shhhhhhhhhh! Her epicurean principles were utterly violated.

Shhhhhhhhhh! Her insistence on purity of ingredients was decimated.

"I hate you!" she gasped, still laughing in spite of her disgust. "You are a vile, unprincipled, terrible pers—"

Pete squirted the nasty stuff into her mouth.

"Aaaaggghh!"

Then, redeeming himself only slightly, he licked it out, giving her a kiss that weakened her knees.

Pete covered every inch of her with blobs and stripes of the Insta-Wip while she continued to protest, only shutting up when he threatened her with a brown plastic bottle of commercial chocolate syrup, too.

She had to admit that she didn't mind the removal process. She didn't mind the spin cycle on the washer, either, when they shoved the sheets into it and Pete decided that she looked irresistible on top.

He kissed her, lifted her down, and led her to the couch

in the living room. "Okay, sit there for a minute and close your eyes, Mel."

"Why?"

"Just close your eyes."

She did.

She heard him moving across the room, then a drawer opening and shutting. Then something small and cold hit her chest just above her cleavage. His hands were warm as they moved her hair aside, brushing the back of her neck.

"There," he said.

Melinda opened her eyes and looked down. "Oh!" She fingered the small disc of gold lying snug against her skin. "Pete..."

It was a sand dollar.

He'd given her a spontaneous gift, for no reason. A lump rose in her throat. He wasn't using her. He wasn't simply having fun at her expense. He actually cared.

"Pete, it's gorgeous. Thank you." She swallowed the lump as she tilted her head back, and he dropped a quick kiss on her mouth. Then he rounded the couch and sat down beside her.

"I thought, since you found one on the beach the night we, um, re-met—"

She chuckled. "That's a nice way to put it."

"Anyway. I thought you might like the necklace."

"I do. I love it. Thank you."

He slid an arm around her and they sprawled, naked and content, while his iPod played Green Day in the background.

A lump rose in Mel's throat as she realized that never in her life before had she sat, naked and unselfconscious, next to anyone. Especially not a man.

She'd always covered herself hastily, with a sheet, a blanket, a robe, a towel—even if she was by herself and emerging from the shower. She'd always had the urge to hide her body, her bulk, her imperfections.

Her eyes filled and her throat ached as she thought about it. She lay her head on Pete's shoulder, though, and let the music and companionship wash over her. The tears gradually faded and so did the ache.

Melinda smiled. She could get used to this...

"Penny for your thoughts," said Pete.

"Not for sale," Mel told him. She squeezed his hand. "Someday, I'll tell you for free, though."

20

THE DAYS CAME AND WENT as Melinda worked on orders for the bakery in the last month before closing her original location and moving to the storefront in Playa Bella. She still hadn't spoken of the move to her parents, and the rift in her relationship with her mother bothered her. But her mother owed her an apology, and it hadn't been forthcoming.

She made a cake shaped like a large wedge of Swiss cheese, with molded sugar-mice playing on and around it. It was for a little girl's birthday.

For a nature-conservancy group, she did a rectangular sheet cake covered with fondant; then added a complete woodland forest scene to the top of it, using wire armatures to support trees built out of gelatin paste with royal icing brushed over the top. She used marzipan to sculpt tree stumps, fallen logs, toadstools, woodchucks, raccoons, rabbits and even gnomes with beards and pointed hats.

Between customers, Scottie helped her do a baby-shower cake with a frilly carriage on top and then an aqua-tinted Sea World cake with sculpted killer whales, dolphins and seals.

And for Mami, she created duck a l'orange bites, garnished with fresh thyme sprinkled over the tangerine-hued icing.

Scottie, enraged, immediately got to work on tiny filet-

flavored mousses. Mel burst out laughing when she found them in the steel industrial refrigerator. "Cheater!" she exclaimed. "These aren't cookies."

"Cheater?" Scottie looked wounded. "No, that would be Low-Down Lyman."

Mel winced. "Sorry." Scottie had caught his boyfriend with someone else recently, which had resulted in huge drama, untold numbers of consolation martinis and an ongoing legal battle over a chair he and the departed Lyman had designed and built together.

The chair had been removed to Mel's townhome for "safe-keeping" (aka spite) while Lyman petitioned to get it back. Since it resembled a futuristic dental recliner that had collided with a hooker's leopard coat, Mel hoped the dispute would be resolved soon. She found it a little disconcerting, especially late at night when she was afraid it would grow fangs and come alive.

She'd blocked the chair from her mind and was working on a cake for the Fraternal Order of Police, shaped like an officer's hat, when the jingle of bells at her bakery door announced a visitor. It was her brother, all six-foot-three of him, dressed in immaculate khaki pants and a white shirt, looking exactly like the handsome young lobbyist that he was.

"Mark!" she exclaimed, and came around the cold case to hug him. "I haven't seen you in forever."

"Too true," said Scottie, who emerged from the back to drool. "Hey, Good Lookin'."

"Beam me up," said Mark, still embracing his sister. He wasn't Scottie's biggest fan.

"Trust me, if I could beam you naked right into my shower stall, I'd do it in a heartbeat."

"Scottie," Mel said in warning tones.

Mark curled his lip. "Don't make me flatten you, little man."

Scottie sighed and fanned himself with a menu. "Oooh. Danger. It always turns me on."

"You'll have to excuse Scottie. He's missing his boyfriend," Mel said pointedly, glaring at him.

"And Mel's missing hers. Check out the new jewelry, Marky-Mark."

Her brother eyed the gold sand dollar around her throat and lifted his eyebrows. "Who's the lucky guy?"

Mel felt her face catch fire. "Nobody," she mumbled, shooting Scottie an "I'll-get-you-for-this-later" look.

"Nobody's giving you some pretty expensive gifts, sis." Mark lounged against the counter with his hands in his pockets. "Do I know him?"

"Nope," she said dismissively. "Want an éclair?"

"Nice change of subject. I'll have a couple of cannoli, please, and a cup of coffee. So who's your beau, Bug-Eyes?"

"Don't call me that, Jerk-Face." God, how easily they slipped into childhood taunts, even decades later. "How's Kendra?"

"Kendra's fine. She gained about five pounds on the honeymoon, though." Mark blithely accepted the plate of cannoli she passed him, clearly not at all concerned about his own caloric intake.

"What a crime," she said dryly. "Did you have her fingerprinted and booked?"

"Funny," her brother said, stuffing his face. "Mom gave her that old recipe for cabbage soup."

"Tasty. Hope you're enjoying that for dinner."

He grimaced. "Are you kidding me? That shit stinks up the whole house."

"I remember the lovely aroma all too well."

"I've been eating at Chipotle on the way home from work."

Mel rolled her eyes as Scottie snickered. "Well, gosh. What newlywed domestic bliss, Marky."

"So who's the guy?" he asked again, impatiently.

"What guy?"

"Mr. Jewelry. Captain Sand Dollar."

"His name is Pete," Scottie said, smirking. "So, Mel, does Pete have a big peter?"

Mark set his plate down with a snap. "Pete? Pete Dale?"

"No!" Mel turned to Scottie. "You are so fired."

"He would have found out anyway," her obnoxious assistant pointed out.

"Yeah? Well he didn't need to find out today!" Mel stole a look at Mark's expression, which was thunderous. "Scottie, get out of my sight or I really will fire you. I'm not kidding."

Scottie vamoosed.

"I'm going to kill him," Mark said, sweeping the remaining cannoli remnants into the trash and tossing his cup of coffee after them.

"You're not killing anyone," Melinda said firmly.

"Yes, I am." Mark shuddered. "If he's buying you jewelry, then he's in your pants. That means I'm going to rip off his head and crap down his—"

"Mark! My pants—and who may or may not be in them—are not your business. So stop." She took a deep breath. "Pete and I, we, um…we reconnected at your wedding, and—"

"I knew it! That lying, conniving sack of shit." Mark's face suffused with red.

"He's not. Pete and I have been dating, okay?"

"Not okay!" Mark shouted. "Out of all the women in Miami, he has to hit on my sister?"

"Stop yelling. He did not 'hit' on me. Pete and I mutually decided to—"

"Ugh!" Mark held out a hand. "Not one more word outta you, Bug-Eyes. I'm going to be sick."

"Don't you think you're having a seriously immature reaction to this? Think about it."

"I don't want to think about it. He's using you, Melinda, and I'm going to make him pay."

"He is not using me, Mark! Why would you automatically assume that? What is wrong with you? What is wrong with Mom, that she'd decide the same thing? God, I really hate you both."

"Mel, you haven't had a lot of experience with men. We're just trying to look out for you."

"Well, stop! I am twenty-five years old, I run a business and I'm capable of living my own life without your interference."

"Fine," snapped Mark. "Then what's next? You gonna bring Pete home for Sunday dinner? Have oatmeal-raisin cookies in the kitchen, just like in junior high?"

Melinda glowered at her perfect brother. "Yes. I think that's a fabulous idea, as a matter of fact. Pete is my…my… boyfriend—"

Was he?

"—and it's time everyone accepted that. I'll set it up with Mom."

"When was the last time you even bothered to call Mom, Melinda? She's really hurt. They haven't seen you since the wedding."

"Right. And have you asked her why? No, I didn't think so."

Mark sighed. "You and Mom need to put your differences behind you."

"We don't have differences. She has a perfectionism disorder, and she needs to keep her mouth shut."

He turned towards the door and pushed it open. "Gee, I can't wait for this little family get-together."

"Me, either. I'll be sure to bring something fattening."

"CAN'T MAKE IT TO dinner that day," Pete said, full-scale alarm igniting on his face. "Sorry."

Melinda paused. "Okay, then how about the following Sunday?"

"Got plans," Pete said, a little desperately. A tic started at the outside corner of his left eye.

"The Sunday after that?"

"No can do." He popped out of her bed like a jack-in-the-box, but she caught his hand and pulled him backward. He sat down heavily on the mattress, his shoulders hunched.

What was wrong with him? Why did his discomfort make her feel nauseous? Did he not want to 'out' their relationship?

She reached for her newfound confidence, confidence that Pete had helped her to find, and pulled it around herself like a blanket. She was being silly. Pete just felt uncomfortable because her mother had been cold to him at the wedding breakfast.

"Pete," she said severely. "You don't have to be afraid of my mother. She doesn't bite."

"You sure about that?"

"Don't be ridiculous. She likes you."

"No. No, I don't think she does. In fact, I'm sure of it, sweetheart."

"Pete, she was frosty to you at the wedding breakfast because I told her that I'd slept with you, and she jumped to the same conclusion Mark did—that it was a one-night stand. Mom disapproves of those."

"You say Mark's going to be there, too? No. Can't do it. I'm pretty sure I'm in the Bahamas that weekend…"

"Honey—"

"And why would you tell your mother that we slept together, right then? Isn't there some kind of code against that? She would have carved off my dick with a butter knife that

morning, by the way, given half the chance. And I don't have any reason to think that she's had a change of heart lately."

"You're overreacting. My mom will be so happy that I have a boyfriend that she'll start adoption proceedings."

Why that should cause an unmistakable shudder to go down Pete's spine, Mel didn't know.

Again, he tried to get up. And again, she tugged him down onto the mattress. "Are you my boyfriend?"

"What?"

She felt like throwing up. "Are you my boyfriend?"

"Yes," he said, after too long a pause. "Of course I am."

"O-kay...?"

"Mel, I have to get home. I've got an early meeting tomorrow morning."

Why was he so resistant to this Sunday dinner? She felt her old insecurities awakening, yawning and stretching. Did Pete not want to officially be her boyfriend? Was he happy to screw her in private, but embarrassed to acknowledge her in public?

"Pete, is there something you're not telling me?"

He turned to stare at her, his gray eyes wide and guileless. "Of course not. Why would you ask that?"

He was lying, and she knew it.

"Is it Mark you're afraid to see?"

"I can't say I'm looking forward to having a fist planted in my eye," he admitted.

"He's not going to do that."

"Yeah? He left an extremely hostile message on my voice mail. Go figure, but I haven't had a moment to call him back."

Mel got out of bed and stood before him naked, hands on her hips. "Pete, this is really stupid. You and I are dating, right?"

"Yeah." His gaze ran appreciatively over her body.

He couldn't fake that, and she felt a tiny bit reassured.

"Then my family needs to accept that, and you need to accept my family. I think a nice way to bridge the gap is for us all to have a Sunday dinner together. So I'm going to ask you one more time—are you available next Sunday?"

Pete wore the expression of a hunted man. He shifted his weight from one butt cheek to another, and then back. He stood up as if the gallows awaited him. "Sure," he said, after a long pause. "Of course. I'd be delighted."

"Great." Mel gave him her most dazzling smile. "I really appreciate it."

"Uh-huh." He fished his boxer briefs off the floor and climbed into them.

What was he keeping from her? She didn't like this, not at all. But half to reassure herself, and half to reassure him, she said, "It's going to be fine."

"Right." He stepped into his pants and pulled them up, then gloomily zipped the fly, slowly and with finality, as if sealing a body bag.

His omission, whatever it was, created a distance between them. And she didn't know how to bridge it. She tried to catch his eye, but he averted his gaze from hers.

Silence stretched between them, a silence that was new and unwelcome.

"What can I bring?" he asked, at last. "A noose?"

21

PETE FELT ACTIVELY SICK on Sunday morning. He really wished that he could punch the dawn back to Saturday night, specifically to the hour when he'd made love to Melinda for what was probably the last time.

You. Are. Going. To. Pay. Peter. Start wondering when the other shoe will drop. Mommie Dearest's words echoed in his brain. When would her killer stiletto clatter to the floor? Surely she'd use this dinner as the perfect backdrop to stage her revenge. It was too much of a temptation for her to resist.

Jocelyn was inhuman, evil, a demon in a dress. He pictured her cackling wildly as she destroyed his life...

And Mel? Oh, God. Mel. She'd come to mean more to him than he'd ever thought possible. He saw her face changing in front of him: the eyes that held laughter, trust, determination and lately, something more—he saw Melinda's eyes go accusatory and cold, like her mother's. The generous, full, curvy lips that he loved to kiss...Pete saw them narrow and flatten, form a straight line of grim disappointment in him. He saw the natural blush in her cheeks intensify to the ruddy red of shame and betrayal.

He had to tell her first. It was that simple. Better that she hear it from him than from her mother.

But the very thought of telling her sickened him. How could he hurt her that way? How could he convince her that he'd never meant to play along? She'd never believe him. And she'd never speak to him again, much less trust him with her heart.

He knew that if he survived this day, that it would kill him. That he'd never again hold her in his arms, stroke the warm expanse of her rosy skin, get lost in the lush invitation of her body.

Though he wanted to lose himself in sleep and denial of what was about to happen, he forced himself to get up, shave, shower and pay some bills.

Pure anxiety had him sweating through his clean shirt, so to kill some more time he re-showered and changed it. Then he paced around his apartment, a caged animal, until it was time to go and pick up Melinda and brave the demon-mother in her professionally decorated circle of hell.

He would tell her.

No, he wouldn't.

Yes, he would.

No. He shook his head. He would not.

And Jocelyn wouldn't, either. No mother could be that vicious, that hurtful, to her own daughter.

Pete convinced himself that he was safe, for the time being. That he still had time to figure out the best approach to this situation. That he could somehow sell his side of things; present it in a better light. After all, he hadn't done anything wrong...

MEL HAD A BUTTER-RUM cake and Mami in tow. She wore dark, dressy jeans cut like trousers, an orange top that made her eyes look even more blue, and high heels that made her ass sway seductively when she walked. If she hadn't been so moody, he might have given it an appreciative squeeze.

But she clip-clopped four paces ahead of him, her chest jutting out like the prow of a battleship, clearly lost in her own aggressive thoughts. Mami's hind legs scrabbled helplessly in the air under her left arm, and even the cake in her right hand seemed to be cowed.

He'd offered to carry something, but Mel said no, seeming to need to hang on to something in each hand. Mami craned her head back to look at him, as if to say, "she's in one of those moods."

"You look nice," Pete said cautiously, as they got into his car.

"I look lacquered," she said.

"Kind of," he said, wondering if this was one of those trick situations where women beat you up whether you agreed or disagreed.

"It's protective armor."

"Oh."

"I need it around my mother."

Pete started to feel sick again.

"Not that you need to worry. It's just mother-daughter stuff."

Heh. If you only knew. "Right. Of course."

They drove in silence for a while, as sweat gathered along Pete's hairline and made an ugly appearance under his arms.

"Melinda, I just want you to know that I really care deeply for you, okay?"

She turned towards him with a frown. "Why does this sound like the beginning of a 'Dear John' speech?"

"What? No! No, it's not meant that way at all."

"Okay. Well, then, I care deeply for you, too, Pete." She smiled, then leaned over and kissed him. "Or I wouldn't hang out with you buck naked. You know that's a big thing for me, right? I've never just sat around nude with anyone in my life."

Pete felt a lump rising in his throat as nausea curled, dense

as fog, in his gut. "I'm glad you feel that comfortable around me, Mel. And I love it. And I'm…weirdly honored…that you can trust me."

"You're different from any guy I've ever met, Fozz. You don't look at me critically. It's like you look at me—I don't know—gratefully."

She was killing him. Absolutely killing him. "I'm always grateful when I'm in the company of a beautiful naked girl." The b-word popped out of his mouth before he could stop it, and she stiffened.

Then, to his surprise, she visibly relaxed her posture. "That's the thing with you, Pete," she said softly. "You really think I'm beautiful."

"I really do," he said. "I'm sorry if you don't like the word."

"It's okay," she said after a pause. "It's okay, because you make me feel beautiful. You're the only guy who ever has."

Pete took one hand off the steering wheel and squeezed hers, hard. He didn't trust himself to speak, especially since he'd just pulled up to the imposing Mediterranean revival house where her parents lived.

Pete stared at the triple-tiered, white-stone fountain in the center of Jocelyn's disciplined landscaping. He wondered if he could drown himself in it before she opened the door.

And then it was too late: Mark and Kendra pulled up in a shiny new Buick Enclave, Mark's jaw stony and his eyes hidden by impenetrably dark Ray-Bans.

Pete got out of the Z4 and rounded it to open the door for Melinda. He took the cake in its plastic carrier, and then gave her a hand as she scrambled out with Mami, who barked at Mark as he emerged from the Enclave.

"You haven't made a hat out of that thing yet?" Mark asked, as he left Kendra to open her own door.

"How can you even say such a thing?" Mel retorted.

Her sister-in-law climbed out, looking a little annoyed as

she juggled two bottles of wine with her purse and shoved the car door closed with a bony elbow.

Mel hugged her, and once Kendra finished fussing over the dog, Pete bussed her cheek, dutifully. "Hi, Kendra. How are you?"

"Thanks so much for the silver fruit bowl," she said. "That was sweet of you."

"Yeah, I'll think of you every time I grab a banana," Mark said, with an edge to his voice. "Been busy lately, huh, Pete?"

"Mark, be nice," Melinda said in warning tones.

Pete stared into the blank blackness of the Ray-Bans. "Slammed. Sorry I haven't had a chance to call you back."

"Why don't you girls go on into the house. We'll follow you in a minute," Mark suggested, arms folded across his chest.

"Why don't you stop behaving like a caveman?" Mel said sweetly. "Or like a dog that's marking a fire hydrant? Even Mami is more subtle."

At that moment the double doors of the house opened and Jocelyn made her appearance, in a navy blue sleeveless dress and another pair of dagger heels. "Hi, kids!" she said brightly, and held out her arms.

Mark was the first to step into them, and he hugged her back with genuine affection. Kendra, too, was warm in her embrace.

Pete fleetingly wondered if he'd imagined the scenes in his office, or the finger like a gun in the small of his back.

Melinda hesitated infinitesimally before stepping into Jocelyn's arms, but her mother gave her no choice, squeezing her tightly and stroking her hair. "We've missed you, honey."

To Pete's surprise, her steely eyes misted over and faded to a soft, silvery-blue. Jocelyn Edgeworth truly loved her daughter. It was evident in her expression; in the way her mouth softened as she kissed Melinda's cheek.

He gaped at the spectacle, and she noticed, meeting his

eyes over Mel's shoulder. Her own were deeply shadowed underneath, despite the careful application of makeup. She looked as if she hadn't slept in a week.

"I've missed you, too, Mom." Melinda's voice caught on the words.

"Pee-ter." Jocelyn disengaged herself from Mel and took his hand. She kissed the air next to his face and he produced a polite smile. So this was how they were going to play it. He allowed himself a small measure of relief.

"How are your parents?" she asked. "Are they still in Alabama? Does your mother still make that divine pecan ring of hers?"

"Fine, thanks, yes, and yes." Would Mrs. E drop her little bomb this evening, or not? Would she put strychnine in his iced-tea first?

"Good, good. Well, come in, everyone—don't stand on the doorstep. Richard! Ri-chaaard! Come help with the drinks, please."

Jocelyn had a vodka-and-sugar-free tonic, Richard a gin-and-tonic, Pete and Mark beer, and Kendra one-third of a glass of pinot grigio mixed with two-thirds seltzer water. Mel noted this with a fixed smile and poured herself a hefty-bordering-on-huge glass of red wine while Pete winked at her.

Soon they were seated out on the patio in back of the house, surrounded by greenery. Hibiscus trees grew in pots, lantana sprawled gracefully out of planters, bougainvillea serenaded the wrought-iron fence around the property. Caladiums greeted everyone cheerfully from the shaded areas. There were bromeliads, too, and orchids everywhere.

It was Richard who had the green thumb, from what Pete recalled. He'd had a little gardening cart with a seat on it, and a set of tools in a built-in compartment. He'd also had a truly dorky pair of aerating sandals—shoes with long spikes on them that he used to walk around the lawn, despite Jocelyn's

mortification. But the crowning touch had been the green rubber knee pads, which the boys had made endless fun of.

Pete still imagined that he used them every morning in front of his wife, bowing his forehead to the polished parquet and saying, "Yes, Mistress."

Pete sipped his Corona and tried to banish the image from his mind. Richard was a good guy. And come to think of it, he didn't remember Jocelyn having such an edge to her when they were kids.

Now she distributed platters among them. One held cubes of fat-free cheese that tasted like, and had the consistency of, rubber. The other held cucumber rounds topped with tiny daubs of lobster salad. Poor Mel watched with something close to loathing as Kendra swept away the lobster with a toothpick and ate only the cucumber.

Jocelyn's face held nothing but understanding and approval for her daughter-in-law. They discussed a new diet fad, while Mel went silent and tossed back her wine, Richard yawned behind his hand and Mark stared balefully at Pete from behind his assassin's shades.

"So, how 'bout those Dolphins?" Pete threw out.

"How 'bout those new Dolphins cheerleaders?" Mark asked. "You notice the redhead?"

Kendra narrowed her eyes on her oblivious husband.

"I never notice any woman but Melinda," Pete said with another wink at her.

She rolled her eyes, but he didn't miss the quirk at the corner of her lips.

Mark snorted and took a long pull of his beer.

Richard cast a reproving glance at him and yawned behind his hand again. He eyed the faux-cheese cubes and cucumber rounds with mild distaste. "Excuse me for a moment." He got up and went into the house.

He emerged after a few minutes with a covered ice bucket.

"Richard, we already have ice out here," said his wife.

"Oh. Well, now we have more. By the way, Joss—where are the limes? I can't find them."

Jocelyn expelled an annoyed breath, got to her feet and tottered inside on her dagger heels. Richard loped past her and sat down with the ice bucket, which he passed to Pete. "Real food inside," he whispered.

Pete lifted the lid and bit back a laugh. Inside were microwaved cocktail weenies and all kinds of boxed fried appetizers: mozzarella sticks, stuffed mushroom caps, sliced loaded potato skins.

They all (except Kendra) mashed an item of their choice into their mouths, and then Richard slid the ice bucket behind a planter and laid a finger across his lips.

Jocelyn came back with sliced limes and kept passing the trays of cucumbers and cheese, growing visibly frustrated as each person took a turn luring her back into the house. Even Kendra asked for some hand lotion.

By the time they all sat down to dinner at the highly polished, formally set table inside, Pete almost felt sorry for the woman. But not for long.

Jocelyn had prepared a traditional roast with potatoes, carrots and sliced onions on the side. She'd also made green beans and biscuits. She heaped Richard's plate with food and a generous portion of gravy, then did the same for Pete and Mark.

On Kendra's plate she put two thin slices of roast, one small potato and a large pile of green beans.

And on Melinda's plate, she parsed out one slice of roast, half a potato, and a small mound of carrots and onions. After a moment of consideration, she added a spoonful of green beans, pushed the butter into the center of the table, and handed the meager portion to her daughter. Biscuits were

evidently off-limits for the women, and out of the question for Mel—as was butter.

Pete felt instant sympathy for her.

"Shall we say grace?" Jocelyn commanded.

So they did.

Melinda got even quieter and drank even more wine, something Pete watched with concern. This seemed to be a trend when she was around her mother.

She ate her food mechanically, leaving the onions on her plate. Not surprisingly, she was finished before anyone else. She eyed the roast longingly and took another sip of wine, seeming to struggle with herself.

Pete cut a piece of beef, swabbed it through the gravy on his plate and then popped it into her mouth.

Jocelyn's eyes narrowed upon him.

He shot her his most engaging grin and lifted his beer to her before drinking.

They all chatted about this and that for a while, before Jocelyn offered seconds to all the men, who gladly took her up on them. Meat, vegetables and biscuits were loaded up a second time, and complimented.

The girls may as well have been invisible.

Pete's sense of outrage grew.

Melinda's jaw worked as she looked down at her empty plate. "May I have another slice of beef, Dad? And Mark, please pass the biscuits." Melinda's voice was serene, but firm. She reached out a hand and pulled the butter dish toward her from the center of the table, as her mother's face blanched in horror.

Yes! Pete wanted to cheer for Mel.

"Sweetheart," Jocelyn admonished, "there's a lot of fat in that roast. And half a cup of butter in the biscuits already!"

Mel continued to put food on her plate. "Correct me if

I'm wrong, Mother, but you invited me to a meal, not a fasting session."

Jocelyn pinched her lips closed, with an expression that suggested it was painful to do so.

All the guys continued to eat, their eyes on the table. But Pete felt choked by the food. These people! Couldn't one of them stand up for Mel?

Kendra looked longingly at the biscuit platter and then away, out the window.

Mel poured gravy onto her meat, then slathered butter on her biscuit. She took a large bite of it, her eyes on her mother.

Twin spots of pink appeared high on Jocelyn's cheeks. She opened her mouth again, but closed it when Richard caught her eye and shook his head.

"No, go ahead, Mom, really," Mel said, with her mouth full. "Tell me how overweight I am. Tell me the exact number of carbs in this biscuit. The number of fat grams. And break down the nutritional content of the gravy, while you're at it."

"Melinda, is the hostility necessary?" Richard asked.

She swallowed her food. "Yes. Yes, actually, it is. Because ignoring her doesn't work. It just eggs her on. And asking her to stop politely doesn't work, either. And nobody else in this family will take my side, or stand up to her. Mom, maybe you should know that Dad has a little freezer in the garage, hidden behind his fishing gear."

Jocelyn gasped in outrage and skewered poor Richard with her eyes. He closed his.

But Melinda wasn't done yet. "Maybe you should clue in that when we were out on the patio, everyone was eating contraband fried food out of the ice bucket! Because people hate your disgusting cheese cubes and cucumber rounds."

Mel put her fork down, took a deep breath and stood up. "Food should be appreciated, not treated like an enemy. Food should be enjoyed, not despised. Meals should bring a fam-

ily together, not drive them apart. So I'm thirty pounds overweight. I am not going to apologize for liking food!"

Utter silence reigned at the dinner table until Pete put down his own fork and applauded.

"I'm FAT," Melinda shouted at her mother. "So what? I'm happy! I am not going to live in misery, with stomach cramps, in order to fit into a pair of size-zero jeans!"

"Melinda," Pete said. "You're not fat." He turned to her family. "She's not. She is the sexiest woman I've ever seen, she's gorgeous, and this family had annihilated her self-esteem when I 're-met' her only a few months ago. That's just wrong, people. And if you can't love her the way she is, well, then…" He stared at each person around the table for a good beat. "If you can't love her the way she is, then I feel sorry for you. But I *do*."

Melinda's mouth trembled. Her eyes filled and spilled over, tears running down her cheeks. "God, I love you, Pete Dale. You are my hero."

22

PETE FOLDED HER into his arms, hugged her tightly and kissed her repeatedly. *Please don't let this be the last time I ever do this.* "I love you, too, Mel. Please remember that."

Jocelyn was trembling with genuine hurt and suppressed fury.

He knew the other shoe was about to drop, and that it was a steel-toed construction boot with a guided missile system. Target: his ass.

"He's not your hero, you stupid, ungrateful girl!" she exclaimed. "And it's your family, it's me who loves you, not Peter Dale—who only called you again as part of a business deal, but seems to have a very selective memory about that."

Richard choked, while Mark and Kendra gasped in unison. Pete froze as the color drained from Melinda's face.

Jocelyn got up and threw her napkin down on the table like a gauntlet. "Why don't you explain to our darling Melinda, Pee-ter?"

"Why don't you explain, Jocelyn?" Pete countered. "And while you're at it, why not elaborate on how you can destroy your daughter just to spite me and get the upper hand in an argument? Why don't you apologize for treating Melinda the way you do?"

Mel looked from Pete's face to her mother's and back to Pete's.

"What exactly is going on here?" Richard demanded.

"I am sorry, Melinda," Jocelyn said unexpectedly. "I truly am. I don't mean to hurt you. I love you…and all I have ever wanted is the best for you."

But it was too little, too late. Mel seemed to barely hear her. She turned to Pete, eyes huge, her expression almost pleading. "What business deal?"

Her mother's face crumpled. "I made a mistake."

"You think?" Pete snapped.

Melinda's breathing had become fast and shallow. A pulse jumped below her jaw as she cut her gaze to her mother again. "What did you do?"

Jocelyn's mouth worked, but evidently she couldn't get the words out, which left the excruciating task to Pete.

He wanted to run, hide from this conflict, slide under the bed or slip out the window as he had so many times as a kid. But he stood his ground for Melinda. If she had to hear it, then she deserved to hear it from him.

He could hear his own heart beat dully in his ears; feel his blood sluggish in his veins, like pudding stuck in a straw. He even had difficulty drawing breath into his unwilling lungs.

"Mel," he said. His very voice sounded foreign to him, probably because he wanted to disown it and disavow what he had to say. "I had every intention of calling you after the wedding. But evidently your mother didn't have faith that I would. So…" He swallowed convulsively. "So she came to me and offered to do all of her charity functions at Playa Bella if I did. Call you, that is."

Melinda's whole body began to tremble as she absorbed the implications of his words.

Pete spoke faster and faster. "I told her that I was planning to call you anyway, but she didn't believe me. My instinct was to throw her out of my office, Melinda—I should have—but I needed that business, and I told myself that it

didn't matter because I was going to call you anyway. So it didn't count as a bribe."

She didn't move a muscle; she simply exhaled an odd little puff of air. It decimated him—he suddenly remembered why people said "God bless you," when someone sneezed: the belief that the soul popped out of the body and could be snatched in an instant by the devil.

He felt that something had left Melinda with that tiny exhalation, something precious that he could never recover for her.

"You're *despicable*."

He barely heard her words; they were so quiet. And yet they were more devastating than a death rattle. "Mel. Oh, God. I swear to you, Melinda, that—"

She turned away, turned to her mother as if in slow motion, and looked her up and down from head to toe, in utter disgust. "And you. There aren't any words bad enough to describe you. You're a sick, unnatural woman."

Jocelyn lowered her head and put her hand out as if to ward off a blow. She no longer looked like a powerful socialite with the tongue of a viper. She looked old and frail and miserable.

Pete would never understand why he said it, but he did. "Mel, she didn't want you to be hurt. I doubt she thought beyond that."

She threw her head back. "Shut up!" she shouted. "So I was your pity-fuck. At least she was smart enough to see it. I was so dumb that I believed your lies and fell for your manipulation."

She was shaking with emotion, her blue eyes raw with betrayal in her stark white face.

"No, Mel. You were never that. Please believe me," Pete pleaded.

"I'll never believe anything that comes out of your mouth again, you son of a bitch."

"Mel, I called you because I wanted to. Mel, I love you."

"Liar! You're still telling everyone what you think they want to hear, Mr. Customer Service. You can't even stop, can you? You soothe, you placate, you suck up, you kiss ass. You make me sick."

Richard got up from the table, went to his daughter, and put his arms around her. Over her shoulder, he inspected his wife as if she were a particularly repulsive species of maggot.

Mel said brokenly, "Dad, take me home. Oh, please…just get me out of here and take me home."

"I'll do that, sweetheart." He eyed Jocelyn somberly. "And I'm not sure I'll be coming back."

Looking pole-axed, she slid down the dining room wall into a navy puddle on the polished floor. She gave a cry of anguish as they left, slamming the garage door behind them.

After a half moment of silence, Mark surged out of his chair, his face and his fists like granite. As Kendra shrieked, he reached across the table and grabbed Pete by the collar, hauling him through the green beans and biscuits. "I'm gonna kill you, shit head."

As flecks of Mark's saliva settled over his face, all Pete felt was bone-weary. He nodded. "You do that, Mark. Go ahead and hit me. I friggin' deserve it."

"You sure as hell do! You pick up my sister at my wedding, use her for sex and then lie to my face about it? You—"

Suddenly Pete's weariness morphed into rage. Without conscious thought, Pete gripped Mark's shoulders and head-butted him, hard, knocking him backward into Jocelyn's loaded china cabinet.

"For the last goddamned time, I didn't use Melinda for sex! Why will you people not get that through your thick heads? Why?"

Mark blinked in shock, then recovered and came for him head down, like a bull. The dining room table went over in a crash of silver, glassware and porcelain and Kendra screamed.

"If you want to know the truth, she came on to me, and I was flattered! I thought she was hot!" Pete yelled the words right before being brutally sandwiched between the floor and two-hundred-forty pounds of pissed-off Mark.

"Don't talk about my sister that way," he panted, and then plowed his fist into Pete's jaw.

"I friggin' love your friggin' sister, you friggin' asshole!" Pete thundered, as he punched Mark in the eye. All the aggression that he'd tamped down and avoided over the years roared out of him. Mark became his brother, his father, and Pete opened up a can of good old-fashioned Whoop-Ass on him, despite the fact that Mark outweighed him by a good thirty-five pounds.

They rolled back and forth on the floor, through scattered utensils and shards of plates and slices of roast.

Mark grabbed Pete by the hair and crushed his face into a mound of onions.

Pete managed to get an arm under Mark and flipped him, then sat on him and rained down punches indiscriminately.

Mark grabbed Pete's nuts and sent him flying into a wall.

Kendra threw a bowl of cold water on them both, which did absolutely no good.

When they finally came to a screeching halt, it wasn't out of fatigue or common sense. It was because Jocelyn had brandished a huge serving fork in their faces and Kendra was threatening, at the top of her lungs, to call 911.

MELINDA CLUTCHED MAMI to her chest as her father drove her back to her townhome in Coconut Grove. She held on to her anger at her mother just as tightly, because if she even gave one thought to Pete right now she'd come apart…and she wasn't a little girl anymore. Richard couldn't pick her up and bandage a skinned knee, or kiss an injured funny bone to make it better.

There was something desolate inside her, a dark fissure that

had opened at Pete's betrayal, scorched along the edges and bottomless in depth. That he was the man she'd trusted enough to bare her soul and her body to…the pain was unbearable.

"Your mother," Richard said quietly, "isn't a bad person."

"She's a witch."

"No, she's not. She's…obsessive about some things."

"That, Dad, is the understatement of the year. She's crazy."

Her father sighed, and dragged a hand through his thinning hair. "Melinda, your mother wasn't always like this. When you and Mark were kids, she ate birthday cake and cookies right along with you. Do you remember?"

"No." But in the far recesses of her consciousness, Mel did have blurry images of Jocelyn licking the chocolate frosting off of the bottom of a big wax candle shaped like the number six. And eating something gooey that Melinda had made in her Easy-Bake Oven in third grade…

Her father tightened his hands on the leather steering-wheel of his Jaguar. "I'm going to tell you something that I never thought I'd share with you, because you won't see me the same way. And I always wanted to be a hero in the eyes of my little girl." He shot her a wry, sad smile.

She couldn't imagine anything that would tarnish his image in her eyes, or explain her mother's personality. But she waited for him to share whatever it was.

"Melinda, this isn't easy for me to say. But when you were about nine, I had an affair. I cheated on your mother with a young woman in my office."

Mel gaped at him.

He nodded. "She was…stunning. To this day I don't know what she saw in me—maybe a man of authority, a man with some money. But she made it very hard to say no, and I was weak. Your mother and I had had the typical marriage problems—fatigue, fights over money, giving up our identities and hobbies to raise you kids. Your mother wanted me to

take out the garbage and mow the lawn, and this other young woman treated me like a god, like a superhero."

Mel closed her eyes. This was really just too much in one night. She didn't want to know any more.

"Your mother found out about the affair, of course. And she took it very hard. I gave up the girl and we saw a marriage counselor, but your mother stopped eating and dyed her hair blond. She underwent some cosmetic procedures that to this day I don't think she needed. And she changed—her whole personality changed."

"Oh, God. She became the cucumber queen."

Richard nodded. "Melinda, she was very, very angry with me, but she refused to show it—I think she was afraid that it would do more damage to the marriage. Instead, she took to blaming herself. If only she hadn't gained weight with her pregnancies. If only she'd kept her nails done. It was crazy and I told her that, but…of course I was the last person she was going to believe. I'm so sorry to this day, honey. I am the reason that your mother is the way she is. I've tried to make it up to her over the years, and she's forgiven me, but she'll never forget."

"That's why she got so angry with me at the wedding, Dad. I understand more, now. She was harping about my weight, and I lashed out at her. I asked if she was afraid to gain an ounce because you might not love her if she did…I guess I didn't even realize how close to the bone I cut that night."

"Honey, she loves you."

"Dad, I don't want to hear it. How could she do what she did? How could any mother do that to her child? It was cruel. It was thoughtless. It was borderline insane."

"I don't know. She worries about you. She worries about your self-esteem."

"And she thought that she'd improve it if she bribed a guy to take me out?!"

"I didn't say she was right. I can't defend what she did. But

I think in some warped way, she was trying to make up for…
things. The negative relationship between you two upsets her."

"Sure—about as much as breaking a nail does."

"That's not fair."

"I can't believe you're defending her!"

"Sweetie, my defense of her doesn't mean a lack of support for you, okay? This isn't a war."

Melinda snorted.

"It really does upset her. She doesn't know how to talk to
you, or be with you, without antagonizing you."

"Really? Gee, I hadn't noticed."

"There's no need to be snotty to me."

Mel leaned her head back against the seat. "I'm sorry."

Her father just squeezed her hand again.

"Are you leaving her?" Melinda got right to the point, as
he pulled the car into her driveway.

He sat silently, with his head bowed. "No. I'm furious at
her, sweetheart. But she stuck by me when I screwed up. And
I'll stick by her."

"Do you love her?"

He nodded. "I do. There are times when I don't want to
love her, but people don't come perfectly assembled in a box,
Melinda. They have flaws. They have warts and personality
streaks that their partners may not always like. The bottom
line is that we are a family, honey. And we love each other."

"Dad, I'm sorry but I can't love her right now. She's
crossed a line."

Richard nodded. He reached out and touched her cheek.
"That's okay. You try to love her again next month."

"I don't know, Dad." But she hugged him, feeling fresh
tears form under her stinging eyelids. "I don't know."

He squeezed her tightly. "Just try. If not for her sake, then
for yours."

23

PETE DRAGGED HIMSELF to a sitting position against Jocelyn Edgeworth's dining room wainscoting, while Mark did the same at the perpendicular wall.

Jocelyn sat in the middle of the floor, sobbing uncontrollably, mascara running in twin rivers down her cheeks and the toasting fork in her lap. One of her expensive shoes dragged in a puddle of gravy, but she didn't appear to notice or care.

Kendra, utterly silent now, handed her a cloth napkin for her face. Then she began to tackle the mess with a dustpan and broom. She was clearly upset with her husband, and didn't offer him so much as an old washcloth for his bruises.

Mark watched her sheepishly. "Uh. I'm sorry, Ken. I just lost it."

"Apologize to him, not me."

"We're guys. We don't do that."

Kendra looked at Pete.

Pete shrugged. "It's true."

"Then apologize to your mother," she said sternly, "for trashing her house."

"I'll get to that. But first, I have to say that was one spectacular meal, Ma." He winced as he fingered his swelling eye. "What do you have planned for dessert?"

Jocelyn's broken sobbing continued unabated.

"Though I gotta tell you, that scene is a tough act to follow." He gingerly fingered his split lower lip and prodded a couple of teeth to see if they were in any danger of falling out.

Pete tried to muster the energy to do the same, but failed.

"Hey, just checking—you didn't bribe Kendra to marry me, did you?"

Jocelyn collapsed onto the floor, her shoulders shaking.

"Mark!" Kendra rebuked him sharply. "Is that necessary?"

He sighed and crawled through the mess to get to his mother. He rubbed her back as she lay there, then eased an arm under her and pulled her upright, into his embrace. She leaned her head on his shoulder, still weeping.

"Look, I'm an ass sometimes. But Ma, what were you thinking?"

Her response was indecipherable; not recognizable as human. She just keened like a wounded animal.

"Okay, okay," Mark said soothingly. "Shh. Shh, Mom. It's going to be all right."

She blubbered something incomprehensible into his shirt.

Pete supposed he should have felt satisfaction, but all he felt was pity for the woman. He was embarrassed by her raw emotion—he felt superfluous, to say the least. He searched for the motivation to get himself up and then out the door to his car. But every part of his body throbbed in agony. And that didn't even begin to describe his psyche.

He'd lost Melinda. For good. There was no coming back from something like this. No forgiveness.

Get up. Get out. Slowly he obeyed his brain's commands and hauled himself upright. "Mrs. E, I won't say it's been a pleasure, exactly, but thank you for having me. Kendra, take care. Mark—"

"Where do you think you're going?" his friend said.

"Home."

"Sit your ass down," said Mark.

"No, keep it standing," his wife ordered. "And you get yours up, *dear*. One of you can get me a contractor bag. The other one can bring a mop and a bucket so I can teach you how to use them. Nobody is leaving this house until this mess is cleaned up and we have a list of china and crystal that we need to replace for Jocelyn. You morons."

Mark's eyebrows shot up.

"Welcome back," Pete said wryly, "from your honeymoon."

Kendra dumped another dustpan load into the trash, as if to say, "Damn straight."

"I'm guessing the garage is still this way?" Pete asked, jerking a thumb toward the back of the house.

"Yeah." Mark groaned as he detached himself from his mother and the floor. "Damn, dude. Where'd you get that right hook?"

"My brother. Let's just say I had plenty of opportunity to study it."

"Huh."

"You ever grab my nuts again, Mark, I will bury you so deep that you'll float up in a Chinese sewer."

"Yeah? You ever straddle mine again, and I'll kick your ass to Baghdad."

"Will the both of you shut up and get poor Jocelyn off the floor? And then get me a contractor bag?" Kendra snapped.

"Sure thing, honey," Mark said. To his credit, he only moaned once as he lifted Mommie Dearest off the parquet and deposited her into a wing chair in the living room.

"And bring me the Ghirardelli bar out of my purse, too. This is no time to be on a diet."

"Yes, ma'am."

"Then get your mother a Xanax and wipe the gravy off her shoes."

Kendra and Pete ended up using a rake in the dining room. He righted the table, then lifted armfuls of gooey mess and plate shards while she held the contractor bag.

"We have to figure out how to fix this," she said quietly.

"Fix it?" Pete repeated. "Fix what? My life? Melinda's?"

"Yes. Not to mention my in-laws' marriage."

"How? I don't think any of it's fixable."

Mark had come back into the room to help. "Do you really love my sister?" he asked Pete gruffly, as he picked up a fallen chair and set it upright.

"How many times do I have to say it?"

"For real. You. And Bug-Eyes." Mark was evidently still having a hard time with the concept.

"Yes. Not that she'll ever talk to me again. And don't call her that."

"How do we get her to talk to Pete again?" Mark asked his wife.

"I don't know," she said wearily. She looked at Pete. "Did you really take a bribe from Jocelyn to call her?"

"No! That's what I keep trying to tell you people. I told Mrs. E. NO. I told her that I was planning on calling Mel anyway. I was really pissed. I even talked to Dev about it."

"Aha! You have a witness," Mark said.

"Well, no. But Dev can testify that I was really hot under the collar about it."

"Dev," Mark said thoughtfully. "You know, if anyone can sweet-talk a woman, it's him."

"But I don't want her to talk to Dev. I want her to talk to me."

"True. Here's the thing, though—Dev is dating Kylie, you know, my aunt? Who's our age?"

"Kylie? The hot blonde who shot him down at the rehearsal dinner?"

"Seems she didn't actually shoot him down. And Kylie is Melinda's best friend. Maybe she can set her straight."

"Set her straight how?"

"Tell her your version of things."

"My version of things is still bad—I did let your mother book her charity events at Playa Bella, instead of telling her to go straight to hell."

"Wouldn't have done any good," Mark said philosophically. "The devil? He wouldn't have let Mom stay. She'd have been trying to redecorate hell, put all the imps and minions on a diet, make him donate to charities."

Pete choked.

Mark winked at him, from his good eye. The other was swollen closed. "Yeah. The devil woulda kicked her out for sure."

"This isn't funny."

"Dude. Just trying to lighten the atmosphere around this place. It's like the world has come to an end. Mom's on Xanax, Kendra's on Ghirardelli, and we're on cleanup duty."

"How's your mother doing?"

"Tried to dial my dad ten times and is hysterical that he won't pick up. I finally took the phone away from her and gave her a killer vodka martini. Now she's somewhere in outer space, heading for a black hole. I'll deal with her when she wakes up."

"I'll deal with her," said Richard, as he walked into the dining room. "Dear God, what happened in here?!"

"Mark and Pete happened in here," Kendra said acidly, as she rescued a headless Lladro shepherdess from the china cabinet, along with a couple of broken porcelain cups. "Mark will be replacing everything he broke," she added, brandishing the shepherdess's broken lamb at him.

He nodded.

Richard looked around in dismay. "Son, this isn't a football stadium!"

"Yeah," Mark muttered, his gaze on the floor. "I lost my temper. I screwed up."

"We're very sorry," Pete interjected. "I'll help with the replacing, too."

"Peter, I must apologize on behalf of my wife. I'm mortified. But I can't say that I'm pleased with your part in things, either."

"Sir, I never meant—"

They all froze as Jocelyn stumbled into the room in her stocking feet, clearly stoned out of her gourd. "Ris-shard? Oh, Rishard. You came back."

"I did," he agreed, eyeing her warily.

She'd cried off all her makeup, and she looked absurdly young and yet a hundred years old simultaneously. "Please forgive m-me. I...I din' want her to feel rejected. I din' want her to feel, ever to feel, l-like I did."

Her husband just stood there, his expression pained, not making a move towards her.

The hand she'd stretched out toward him dropped, and, unsteady on her feet, she clung to the doorjamb for support. "I din' want her to feel...used an' thrown away."

Mark frowned. "Ma, what are you talking about?"

But she just stood there, swaying, eyeing her husband.

An excruciating silence followed. Pete had the uneasy sensation that the lid on a family Pandora's Box had just been pried open, and he didn't want to be around when the rest of the awful secrets flew out to torment everyone.

He opened his mouth to make his excuses, feeling that it was long past time he got out of Dodge.

Then Jocelyn lost her feeble grip on the doorframe and her consciousness. She toppled forward, and Richard instinctively stepped forward to catch her.

24

MELINDA HADN'T EATEN in forty-eight hours, despite the turn-about of her cursed Inner Drill Sergeant, who urged her to do so, and tried to tempt her with Dove ice-cream bars. She told him where to go, as usual.

She'd tried to call Kylie twice, but she'd been unable to reach her. Cryptic Kylie had become Scarce Kylie.

Mel cried into the batter of a chocolate groom's cake and had to throw it out and start over. She wept into the straw-berry icing of a sweet-sixteen cake, too, with the same re-sults. And she dissolved the head of a little yellow marzipan duck for a shower cake, also with tears.

That was all on Monday, while she hid in the back of her shop and made Scottie deal with customers. On Tuesday, he found her flooding the order book, smearing the details and endangering the receipts.

"Okay, I'm doing an intervention, here," he announced.

She was tucked sideways into her chair, barefoot, clutching Mami like a tiny canine life raft while the poor dog looked bewildered.

"It's either that or build an ark. You're raining on Mami's head, did you realize?"

Mel sniffed and looked down. Her dog's head was soaked,

her little mane matted with salt water. Mami twirled in her lap, put her paws up on Mel's chest and licked her chin and cheek.

"At least Mami loves me," she said brokenly. "Oh, Scottie," she wailed, "how could he do it?"

"Who? Oh, him. You know, if you'd take one of his phone calls, you could ask him. But as long as you're not speaking to him, there will be some communication problems. Know what I mean? It's inevitable."

"H-h-hate him," Mel said, into Mami's fur.

"Don't tell me that. Tell him. To be honest, I'm starting to feel sorry for the guy."

"Don't you dare. You're on my side. I pay you, remember?"

"Very true. But Melly, you do not pay me enough to deal with your mother."

"Just hang up on the witch!"

"Yeah…I would, but she's here in person and she's refusing to leave until she's seen you."

"Call the cops and have her hauled off the premises in chains."

"The cops have better things to do."

"She's a menace to society. Seriously, have her arrested."

"Melinda, I can't do that."

"As your boss, I'm ordering you to."

"Mel, you have to talk to her at some point," Scottie said reasonably.

"Do not."

"You sound like a little kid. Grow up, boss."

"Please make her go away," Mel whined. "I'll give you a raise if you do."

"I'm still waiting for the last one you promised me, so no offense, but I don't believe you. Now, man up and go talk to your mother, missy."

"Sic 'im, Mami," Mel ordered her dog. "Gnaw off his toes."

Mami jumped down and ran to Scottie. She sat up on her hind legs and begged. He gave her a cat-shaped biscuit iced in orange-and-white, complete with green eyes and black licorice whiskers.

Mami lost no time in eating it, tail first.

"I'm surrounded by traitors," Melinda moaned.

"Mel, I do have sympathy for you, really. But you need to get up and go face your mother."

Slowly, Mel twisted in the chair and put her feet on the floor, slipping them into the padded clogs she wore at the shop. She had a hard time forcing herself to get up.

"Now!" Scottie ordered. Evidently this was tough leprechaun love.

"Jeez. Okay, okay." Mel grabbed a clean tea towel and mopped at her face. "Can you send her out back, though? I can't deal with her in front of customers."

In back of the bakery, in the little alleyway where the retail shops in the strip mall took deliveries, Melinda had placed a small café table and two chairs. She didn't want to encourage her mother to stay, though, so she stood near them, leaning against the wall with her arms folded across her chest as Jocelyn made her approach.

"Why are you bothering me at work?" she asked rudely.

"Because you haven't left me any choice. I can't get through the gate at your town house and you won't answer the phone when I call. You ignore texts and emails. So I'm here."

Her mom looked frail, and it was evident that she, too, had been crying behind the huge, Jackie-O style sunglasses she wore. Her nose was red and raw; she'd bitten off her pinky-brown lipstick. And horror! Jocelyn had applied her foundation hastily and sloppily—Mel could see a beige line demarcating her chin from her neck.

"The question is, why are you here? I don't have anything to say to you."

"I have something to say to you." She gestured at one of the wrought-iron chairs. "May I sit?"

"If you insist."

With a sigh, Jocelyn lowered herself into the seat, rubbing absently at a blue vein in her hand. "I'm not sure where to start."

Mel eyed her stonily.

"Melinda, I don't mean to be the food police. Wait, let me rephrase that. I have meant to be the food police, but my motives didn't stem from wanting to criticize you. They stemmed from wanting to protect you. The truth is that your father had an affair a number of years ago—"

"Yes, he told me."

"He told you?"

Mel nodded.

Her mother looked nonplussed. "Well. All right. Well. I was devastated. I thought that he'd had the affair because I was fat, because I'd gained weight when I had Mark and you. And I became obsessive. I looked at the women whom your father's contemporaries married after their first wives, and they were all thin, all pretty and well-maintained."

"I get it, Mom. What I don't get is—"

"Just hear me out. Fast-forward to Mark's wedding. I had said nasty things to you when you told me you'd, ah, been with Peter."

"He doesn't go by Peter anymore. He's Pete." Mel wondered why she cared enough to point that out.

"Pete. Fine. Anyhow. I'd said awful things to you, things which I very much regretted. But I couldn't unsay them. And I felt fiercely defensive of you, my darling daughter, and very suspicious of Pete's motives. I wanted to let him know that he wasn't going to get away with using you—and I also wanted to do something to make up for my assault on your self-esteem."

"Make up for it?" Mel repeated scathingly. "Or make it a hundred times worse?"

"Darling girl, I regret what I did with all my heart. It was wrong, on so many levels. I'm sorry."

"Mom, the words don't change what you did. And they don't change what Pete did, either."

"I know that I can't say 'sorry' and make it all better. But I haven't really come on my behalf. I've come on Pete's."

"Oh, please. This should be good."

"You need to know that he did say no. That he did tell me that he was going to call you anyway. I rode right over him. I simply assumed that he was being polite, but I don't think he was. He was angry, Melinda. He wanted to throw me out a window."

"Big deal. He still took the bribe."

"I'm not sure I left him a lot of choice, honey. In all fairness, it is his job to bring in business for that hotel."

"Don't make me sick."

"I think he truly loves you."

"Right."

"After you and Daddy left, Mark attacked him. He hauled him over the dining room table and they destroyed things while going for each other's throats. And he kept yelling—Pete did—that he loved you, and why couldn't anyone get that through their heads?"

Mel felt her face crumpling, and resisted fiercely. She wasn't going to cry in front of her mother. She especially wasn't going to let Jocelyn see that her words had given her any kind of hope. She told herself not to be stupid.

"He's a good man, Melinda. He stayed to clean up. He was agonized about his part in the whole thing, and let your father reprimand him. I really think he loves you, darling."

"Love? What would you know about love?" Maybe it was wrong, especially in light of the fact that her mother was here

to apologize, but all Melinda wanted to do was hurt her as badly as she'd been hurt.

"What would I know about it? Well, you think about this, I loved your father enough to stay with him after he'd betrayed me for another woman. I could have walked out, taken him to the cleaners and deprived him of his children. He certainly deserved it. But I loved him. He was my husband and we'd built a life together. So I swallowed my pride and my hurt and I let him come home…I worked on trying to forgive him. I love your father more than the air I breathe. He's my rock. He's my reason for living. Maybe it's not always easy for you kids to see that. But it's true."

In the face of Melinda's unforgiving silence, Jocelyn got up and hitched her purse over her shoulder. "You don't have to forgive me. I understand that it may take a very long time for you to even think about it. But I do think that you should give Pete a chance to explain to you, to make it up to you, and to love you."

She touched Mel's shoulder, and Mel did her best not to recoil. "Thank you for at least letting me talk…letting me apologize." Jocelyn turned and walked away, back down the little alley, toward the parking lot where she'd left her car.

Melinda watched her go. She couldn't tell her that everything was okay between them. She couldn't yet forgive her. But she did recognize that it hadn't been easy for her mother to come here, to talk about the past and old wounds, or to plead the case of a man who had every reason to hate her.

She'd done it out of love, plain and simple—even if that love was buried deep under Botox and St. John knits, under compulsive dieting and Valentino handbags. She deserved an acknowledgement of that, some kind of crumb.

"Hey, Mom," Melinda called. "You want to come inside for an oatmeal-raisin cookie?"

Okay, so it was a test. She admitted it. Was her mother

up to the challenge? Would she ingest actual calories in the name of peace?

Jocelyn stopped in her tracks. Put her hand to the strap of her bag. And turned around. She walked three steps back toward her daughter. And her voice trembled as she said, "Yes, Melinda. Thank you. I'd love an oatmeal-raisin cookie."

25

PETE WAS BONE-WEARY as he met with his boss on Wednesday. They stood in Pete's office, a small miracle, since usually Rafi made his employees come to him.

Pete went through the motions, listening with half an ear and responding with half a brain. Since the debacle at the Edgeworths' home; since losing Melinda, he couldn't make himself care about anything at all.

He'd gone from pleasing everyone to pleasing no one. He'd gone from aboveboard to downright manipulative and Machiavellian. He'd gone from pacifist to brawler. The bottom line? He no longer knew who he was anymore. He was only conscious of being a sad sack of shit who'd hurt the woman he loved, and in the process, destroyed his life.

Reynaldo's petty concerns held no interest for him. He only wanted to get his desk and phone back from his boss, so that he could try calling Melinda yet once more.

Not that she would answer.

He'd apologized on her voice mail until he was hoarse. Begged her to at least give him a chance to explain. He'd even enlisted the leprechaun's aid, to no avail. She wouldn't see reason, much less Pete.

He was done. Someone needed to stick a fork into him.

"Pedro! I asked you a question," Reynaldo snapped.

Pete blinked at him. "Sorry. What was that?"

"How many events has Gareth Alston booked here for Governor Vargas?" Reynaldo asked.

"Four. Two fundraising dinners, a ball and a luncheon."

Reynaldo's eyebrows shot up and his mouth opened, releasing his unlit cigar into his lap. "You have done well, my friend. Clearly you made Gary quite happy." He winked and dug the cancer stick out of his crotch, then waved it. "You swing both ways, my friend?"

Pete bit down hard on an unwise retort.

"No, Rafi, I do not. You know better. But I did introduce Alston to his new squeeze, Scottie, a couple of weeks back. Evidently they've been tearing up the town—and the Bal Harbour shops—together.

Reynaldo snorted. "*Maricones,*" he said, in dismissive tones.

Pete gritted his teeth.

"Now. The bakery," said his boss. "I do not like the colors. I do not like the, how you say? The logo. And no café seating outside of the shop—Playa Bella is not a Parisian sidewalk."

Great. Wonderful. And how was he to deliver that message to Melinda?

"Pedro, what happened to your face? Were you in a fight?"

"Me?" Pete asked. "No, no. I got hit with a baseball over the weekend."

"This baseball, it got you in the ribs as well as the jaw? Because you are moving like an old man."

"Arthritis," Pete said.

"Indeed? In one so young. A shame."

Pete didn't give him an inch. His personal life was none of his boss's business.

"So," Reynaldo said, "you will inform Ms. Edgeworth that

she will change the paint colors in the storefront, and that we will work with her on modifications to the logo. Also—"

Pete cleared his throat. "According to her contract, Melinda has the right to make design decisions for the boutique space."

Reynaldo waved that famously dismissive right hand of his. "Playa Bella is my hotel. Her business must work within the existing space."

"I think she and the architect tried very hard to honor that, Rafi."

"I don't like the colors," his boss repeated. "They will be changed."

"Well, I'll speak to Melinda about it, but—"

"No buts. And the logo—it must be more formal, more stylized. This is too casual."

"Sir, I believe she's already ordered all the bags, boxes, stationery and labels with this logo on them."

Reynaldo guillotined the end of his cigar with his platinum cutter. "This is my problem why?"

"Again, according to her contract, she has the right—"

"This is my hotel," Reynaldo repeated. "She must work with me, according to my preferences." He walked to Pete's desk and riffled through some files, without excusing his nosiness or invasion of privacy. "Ah. And here is the pilot script for the television show. I will approve it, with some small changes, but there is a larger issue."

"Oh?"

"I have spoken with the prospective producers, and they agree that she is quite pretty, but she's *gorda*. She must lose some weight. Tell her."

Pete opened and then closed his mouth. "You want me to tell her that she has to lose weight?"

"*Si*, Pedro. Are you deaf?"

Pete eyed him with long-suppressed loathing. He'd had it. Mr. Nice Guy? He was leaving the building.

"My name is Pete, Rafi. Please don't call me Pedro." He said it calmly, however, keeping the edge out of his voice.

His boss looked up from the file, one eyebrow raised. "*Perdón,* Pete. You have never objected before."

"Yeah. Well. I'm objecting now. Another thing, Rafi— I'll speak with Melinda about the colors and the logo, but you should know that she has the legal right to keep what she's chosen."

"And you know what to do if she proves stubborn. Cancel her contract."

"That would be cutting off your nose to spite your face, sir. You'd have to release the space. Build it out all over again. The storefront will sit empty for months, especially in this economy."

"It's your job, Pete, to make sure that I don't have to deal with that. Get her to make the changes."

"I'll do my best."

"And get the girl on a diet."

"About that." Pete fought to hang on to his long-dormant temper. "I think Melinda Edgeworth is a beautiful woman. I don't think she needs to lose weight."

Reynaldo's small black eyes gleamed with malice. "Did I ask you what you think, Pete? No, I did not. I asked you to pass along a message to her, one that comes straight from the producers."

"And I'm telling you that I won't do that, Rafi. It will hurt her unnecessarily and I refuse."

His boss's face turned a mottled red, almost purple. "I'm giving you a direct order!"

Pete saw his career flash before his eyes. He thought about the horrible economy and how long it might take him to find another decent job. He thought about the possibility that when that job offer came, he might have to move out of Miami to take it.

Then he thought about Melinda, whom he'd already devastated. He pictured her face as he delivered the message from yet another source that she needed to lose weight in order to please someone. And he made his decision.

"That's a direct order that I must respectfully decline to accept."

"You are making a very big mistake, my friend."

"So be it."

"Then you're fired, Pedro. *Comprendes?* Fired. Get out."

Pete nodded. "I'll pack my things. And for the last friggin' time, don't call me Pedro."

Reynaldo picked up the phone on his desk, hit zero, and barked into the receiver. "Security! I need you to escort a man from the premises."

Pete opened a couple of desk drawers and removed some personal items. He took the photos of his mother and his college friends off the windowsill. He dropped everything into his computer bag and left the laptop itself on the credenza.

"Not necessary, Rafi. I'll leave under my own steam. But just to let you know? I wouldn't tangle with Ms. Edgeworth and her contract. You may find that she didn't agree with certain clauses in it, and struck them out."

MELINDA SAT, POLEAXED, outside Pete's office as he put an end to his career at Playa Bella—for her. That hadn't been Mr. Customer Service in there. Not Mr. Professional Suck-Up. Not Mr. Nice Guy.

That had been a man standing up for the woman he loved, just as he'd stood up for her against her family at Sunday dinner.

She couldn't even speak as he walked purposefully out of the room without looking back, his computer bag slung over one shoulder. He never saw her, and she didn't know how to call him back or what to say.

But she realized in that moment that he was the One. The man she'd been waiting for all her life had been teasing and tormenting her since junior high. He'd called her names and buried her in the sand and trapped her in a tree house. And somehow, that terrible kid had grown into a good man, and he'd developed true gallantry.

As Mel watched her white knight make his exit, she could hear the dragon he'd slain for her still floundering around his office. She smiled to herself as she heard him pick up the phone and bark at his attorney to review her contract.

She stood up as two uniformed security guards surged toward the door. The dragon needed to hear what she had to say.

Mel walked into Pete's former office, her head held high. "Mr. Reynaldo, I'd like to say something to you."

He gave her a black look. "Not now."

"Yes," she said. "Now. You need to know that I will not change the paint colors or the logo I've chosen for the bakery here in Playa Bella. You should also know that I am perfectly satisfied with my looks and my weight, and my opinion is the only one that matters. I will not go on a diet for the cable TV program. I won't go on a diet for anything, or anyone, except myself—if and when I decide to do so. Are we clear, Mr. Reynaldo?"

The security guards hovered at the door. Mel was quite sure she'd be leaving between them, each man gripping one of her upper arms and propelling her down the hallway. She waited for Reynaldo to order her off the premises.

But he simply pulled the cigar from his mouth, growled something under his breath and gave her a blank stare. "*Perdón*, Ms. Edgeworth, but I do not know what you're talking about. I do not know what you think you heard, but it wasn't about you."

Melinda should have known. Without an employee to bully and to hide behind, the man was all talk.

"Why should you lose weight?" Reynaldo asked her, giving her an oily smile and gesturing with his cigar. "You are a lovely young lady with impeccable taste, and we are very fortunate to have you working with us here at Playa Bella." He took her elbow and escorted her into the hallway, ignoring the security guards. "Walk with me, eh, and let us discuss a few details of your upcoming baking program…"

26

PETE HADN'T LEFT the premises. Melinda knew that because his car was still in the parking lot after she finished her nauseating little chat with Reynaldo. Thank God she wouldn't have to interact with him every day—she'd have her own space and run it as she saw fit. She had a feeling that thanks to Pete, Reynaldo's lawyer was going to tell him to back off.

If Pete wasn't in his office and he wasn't in the parking lot, then that left two other possibilities. He was either in the bar or walking on the beach.

Mel headed through the marble-floored lobby with its colossal floral arrangement, past the grand piano and the fountain in the center of the rotunda, and into the dark wood-paneled bar with its leather stools and mounted trophy fish, where there was no sign of Pete.

She pushed through the double doors that gave access to Playa Bella's private beach, and there he was, walking along the shore barefoot with his pants rolled up to his knees.

He'd rolled up the sleeves of his blue business shirt as well, and it flapped, untucked, in the ocean breeze.

The warm, humid, salt-tinged air washed over her face and she took a moment to appreciate it, along with the sky so blue it almost looked artificial. Not a cloud was in sight,

only a few gulls floating on the air currents and basking in the generous rays of the afternoon sun.

Melinda slipped off her sandals and left them by the hotel doors. As she walked across the sand, her long, flowing skirt flew crazily in the wind, plastered against her legs one moment and lifting above her knees the next.

There was something elemental about walking in sand; something that reminded her, as her toes slid in and out of it and her heels sank unexpectedly, that life was earthy and uneven, that she had to adapt and shift with it.

Pete stood with his hands shoved deep into his pockets, his gaze fixated on the horizon, and didn't notice her approach until she reached out and touched his arm.

"Mel!" he exclaimed, startled. "What are you doing out here?"

She looked up into those steady, kind gray eyes of his. "Looking for you."

"Why?"

She dug a toe into the sand and smiled. "To ask you to dance."

His breath hitched. Clearly he remembered the night of Mark's wedding; the words he'd said to her on this very beach. He went completely still as his eyes searched her face. Then his own split into a grin. He took a step closer to her and settled his hands on her shoulders. "You forgive me?"

She shrugged.

"Mel, I never meant to say yes to that deal with your mother. I'm so sorry—you have to believe me—it wasn't like that on my part. I figured she could think whatever she wanted, but I'd know the truth."

"I do believe you."

"And for what it's worth, she didn't do it to hurt you. She did it, however bizarre this sounds, to protect you from being hurt."

"I know that, now. She's bent in some weird places, but she didn't mean any harm." She reached up to touch his bruised, abraded jaw. "I'm sorry that Mark did this."

"Ha," Pete said. "He looks a lot worse."

The old "Have you seen the other guy?" line. Men. "I'm sure he does," Mel said diplomatically.

"I do owe you a huge apology, for even seeming to go along with your mother. I owe you one for not telling her to take her functions somewhere else. But the bottom line is that it was business, and my job was to get more of it."

"I owe you an apology for assuming the worst," Mel said slowly.

They stood for a couple of moments, looking out at the water while the waves lapped at the shoreline. Then Melinda became aware that Pete was studying her. And judging by the bulge at his fly, he liked what he saw.

She glanced quickly away from his fly, but not quickly enough; he noticed that she'd noticed.

Pete gave her a wry grin. "What you do to me," he murmured. "Only you."

"If we had somewhere to go, I'd offer to help you with that."

"I wish I had a room key," he said. "But all I've got is a pink slip."

"I know. I was right outside your office. I heard everything." Tears sprang to her eyes. "Thank you."

"Melinda." He rubbed the back of his neck with evident embarrassment. "That's totally unnecessary. I hope you know that."

"But I need to say it. That's twice now that you've been my hero."

"I'm no hero."

"To me you are. Pete, I'm so sorry about your job."

"I'm not," he said firmly. "Reynaldo was out of line, he's sleazy and I'm tired of being his yes-man."

She peered up at him, a little shy. "So…want to be mine, instead?"

Pete laughed. "Is that an offer of employment or an indecent proposal?"

"Definitely," said Mel, "an indecent proposal."

"All right, then. I accept."

He slid his hands up into her hair and cupped her face as he bent to kiss her. She opened to him and welcomed him, pressing all of herself against him without reservation.

"I love you, Melinda. I love your face, I love your body, I love your heart and your spirit. I even love the way you tore me a new asshole on Sunday night."

She let out an awkward laugh. "Oh, Pete. I love you, too."

He took her hand and they continued to walk along the shore, feet seeking a path through the shifting sand while the breeze picked up and the sun slipped lower in the sky.

She could feel Pete's love for her in the way he squeezed her fingers, the way he brushed flyaway tendrils of her hair out of her eyes, the way he kissed her, ever so gently, with the barest touch of his lips to hers.

He really did love her.

And for once, she couldn't hate her mother for being right.

Epilogue

EVER SINCE REYNALDO had thought about the money Pete made him, eaten crow, offered him a raise and asked him to stay, Pete and Melinda had seen blessedly little of the man. He'd moved on to yet another wife and was busy developing another luxury hotel, this one on South Beach.

All of Mark's wedding party sat, one year later, at a long white-clothed dinner table on the beach behind Playa Bella, enjoying the sunset, the feel of the sand between their bare toes, and the balmy breeze. The roar of the ocean behind them almost drowned out the congratulatory toasts.

Pete's voice held amusement as he said, "To Mark and Kendra on your one-year anniversary. God only knows how she'll put up with you, Mark, for another year..."

Mark had the grace to blush, and he caught his very pregnant wife around the waist. He pulled her in for a hug. "Have the rest of my lobster," he urged her. "You're eating for two now." Then he stood up and raised his glass to everyone, while she took him at his word and dug in.

"Kudos to Adam, our smartest groomsman, for graduating from medical school and getting an internship at M.D. Anderson! Maybe one day, sweet Nikki will make an honest man out of you."

"Thanks," Adam said wryly, and brushed stray sand particles off the lenses of his glasses. "Thank you very much."

Nikki laughed, her corkscrew curls wild in the ocean

breeze. She'd popped out of Mark's cake at the bachelor party and into Adam's life. "I don't know. I'm pretty busy with my new business, but he could make a good starter husband. We'll see."

"Starter? Starter husband?" Adam dug his fingers into Nikki's ribs and she fell off her chair laughing and into the sand, as she tried to escape. "That's keeper husband, babe."

"Right! That's what I meant…"

Adam released her and brushed off his pants. "Now, where were we?" He fixed his gaze on Devon, who had pulled Kylie into his lap. "Hey! Hands on the table, Dev. We'll have none of that hanky-panky you're famous for."

"Who, *moi?*"

"Yeah, you. We're all very pissed that you chose to elope to Greece to get married, depriving us of the spectacle of the century, and the bachelor party of the millennium. And we'll never understand what Kylie sees in you, not ever. But we have arranged, this very night, to get you back for every terrible thing you've ever done to us."

"Everything?" Dev asked, a mocking grin playing around his mouth.

"Yep," Adam reiterated. "Everything. So stand up."

Dev stood, cocky as hell, not even bothering to be wary. "Hit me."

"Devster, you really need to pay more attention to things going on around you. Why is it, for example, that your wife is drinking ginger ale, not champagne?"

Dev went a little pale. Then he raised an eyebrow and slowly turned to face Kylie, who aimed a beatific smile at him.

"And why is it," Adam continued, "that she has started not one, not two, but three educational trusts at Sol Bank in the last week?"

Dev blinked. "Th-three?"